The Rekindler

Truth has a price, but a kindle sets a blaze.

Chiara Talluto

Copyright

ALL RIGHTS RESERVED

The Rekindler © 2023 by Chiara Talluto.

Library of Congress Control Number: 2023921277

ISBN: (Paperback) 978-1-7348237-4-5;
(ebook) 978-1-7348237-5-2

Praises

"The Rekindler weaves a story of faith, perseverance, and hope in the face of adversity. The characters, particularly Benjamin Morris, are well-developed and relatable.... Explores the importance of faith and the power of religious conviction in inspiring people to fight for their beliefs.... A dystopian world that feels both unsettling and believable.... Complex themes of religious freedom, persecution, and the resilience of faith with depth and sensitivity.... Pacing keeps the reader engaged.... Suspense builds as the characters navigate the challenges of their mission." ~Natalie Soine, Readers' Favorite, **5-Star Review**

"Chiara Talluto's short story, The Rekindler, is a thought-provoking what-if warning to all Christians. Fast-forward to 2032, the world has undergone a major upheaval, surviving a war that decimated most of the population several years prior. Governments and countries have collapsed and religious freedom is history. To establish order, UNO, a one-world government exists and KASTAM is the only recognized religion. Defy them at your peril. But Benjamin Morris and a small band of staunch Christians have other plans to restore the USA and the rest of the world one person at a time. So begins The Rekindler, a nudge to perhaps make people wake up and pay attention to what's really going on around them." ~Dennis De Rose

Dedication

For my Heavenly Father!

"Sow for yourselves righteousness; Reap in mercy;
Break up your fallow ground, For it is time to seek the Lord,
Till He comes and rains righteousness on you." (*Hosea 10:12*)

Contents

A Tidbit

Dear Reader,

Merriam Webster defines rekindle as "to start or stir up" (something again). The Bible tells us that rekindle means to revive, to bring back to a spiritual life.

A rekindler is a transformed person walking and upholding the things of God, living righteously and graciously. (*1 Timothy 2*)

A rekindler is anyone willing to risk telling the truth for the greater good amidst censorship and freedoms that have been taken away.

Sometimes, God lets us fall more than once in order to pick us up again. Truth always has a price, but a little fire can kindle an entire forest. (*James 3:5*).

Are you a Rekindler?

Chapter 1 – The Assembling

May 2032. Somewhere in Illinois.

Seventy miles from Chicago in an abandoned bricked ranch, concealed by four aging weeping willows, shadowy lights danced, hidden by a heavily draped front window.

Five fold-up chairs were arranged in a half-circle, facing a back-supporting barstool. Four candles in their holders were positioned around the room, flickering to the methodical movements of the seated enigmatic figures.

Sixty-two-year-old former Marine, Captain Benjamin Morris, shifted his husky frame on the high-topped chair, trying to get comfortable. Taking his clipboard and flipping to a clean page on the yellow pad, he jotted some notes, and gazed expectantly at the newest recruits, the majority in their early twenties. "Are you taking precautions wherever you go?"

This was their fourth location move in the last several weeks. Secrecy was a top priority for their safety and Benjamin was compelled to remind them once again the importance of being discreet. Encrypted communication was always sent to their devices no earlier than the day before their scheduled meetings as a safeguard.

"Yes Mr. Morris," Petra answered. An enthusiastic Slavic, twenty-two-year-old brunette college student, excited to absorb her leader's teachings.

Benjamin cleared his throat. "What did I tell you in the previous meetings about not calling me 'Mister Morris'? I am your mentor, teacher, leader, and captain. Call me Captain, Benjamin, Morris, or Sir. Do I make myself clear?"

Petra nervously nodded along with the others, quickly looking down, and reviewing the points she took from the last session. *Acts 2:1-47, commencement of Pentecost, ten days after Jesus ascended into Heaven. Disciples and many other men from other nations gathered, filled with the Holy Spirit, spoke in tongues, prophesized. Chapter ends with Peter reciting Joel's sermon, three-thousand people saved and baptized.*

Morris waited for another reply, "Next."

"All good, sir," replied Jacob, a twenty-year-old Canadian poker player shuffling a deck of cards between his hands.

"Yes, got it," Caleb said, tossing back his head, flipping his red curly hair away from his ears. At eighteen, he was the youngest of this newly formed unit.

"Careful as I can be," Joshua piped up. He was twenty-four years of age, a recent transplant from California. Bronzed, he flexed his bulging muscles through a tight-fitted T-shirt.

Benjamin scratched his cropped salt-and-pepper hair. He peered at the last, silent one in his young squad, "What about you, Franklin?"

Franklin's dark-eyes bulged through black-rimmed frames; he squirmed uncomfortably in his seat knowing his teacher was keeping close tabs on him. *Why does he keep staring at me like that?* At twenty-eight, Franklin had the youthfulness of a seventeen-year-old with long greasy brown hair. Putting a gadget in his back-pocket, he coyly remarked, "Yeah, yeah, I'm safe. I'm not dumb, you know."

Morris slid off his seat and balanced on his left-leg, his bad leg, the one where twenty years earlier, UNO, the new government's militants had beaten him for protesting against President Kirby Borsta at a political rally. Today, two-long scars, thanks to thirty-six stitches, ran from his mid-thigh down to his ankle, a reminder that the cost of one's faith and freedom was a hefty price to pay. A dull pain slinked down his calf; gritting his teeth, he leaned back on the stool for support.

Benjamin glared at his oldest member, "Eyeballs on me, Franklin. What's that supposed to mean? Our safety is vital for our survival. If you're not serious about what we've been doing, I suggest you leave now!"

Franklin held up his hands, "You're right. I'm sorry. I am as dedicated as anyone here," he said pointing to the others, and locking eyes with Petra.

Morris observed something between the two but chose to put it off for the moment. He'd have to have a 'man-to-man' conversation with Franklin later about having more than "*friendly*" relationships on these teams; prohibited because of the dangerous assignments. He had already lost two recruits, Ruth and Paul, who were in his third group; killed execution-style at a café in Los Angeles. Romance had clouded their focus on the job. He vowed after that incident there would be no more intimate affairs, everything strictly platonic.

"Very well. Don't do it again."

Benjamin was aware of Franklin's cocky attitude at times, but he had come through with results. *I can trust him; it's his attitude that needs adjusting.* He was a construction worker by trade. The two met at a site in downtown Chicago, where Morris convinced him to be part of his crew.

He recalled the man's bravery in the last job five weeks earlier in Springfield. UNO was using three warehouse buildings along Interstate 65 as future prison camps for "unruly citizens". Franklin stole the design plans outlining the cells, torture rooms and interrogation areas. Working with Joshua who was employed with an online news and media company, they leaked the documents to the public. UNO had since withdrew out of the development.

Turning to the rest of the crew, he said, "We're accounted for."

"Yes, sir!" the colleagues replied with gusto.

Their leader bowed his head, "Let's pray before this evening's session. Dear Heavenly Father, thank you for this gathering. Fill us with Your wisdom to continue to do Your work. Give us strength, Lord. Protect us, Lord, keep us safe from harm. We do all this in Your Name, Jesus Christ. Amen."

"Amen," everyone murmured.

"What's happening on the ground? Who wants to go first?"

Joshua signaled with his hand, "I will." Stretching his forearms, he flattened out the creases of the piece of paper in his hand. "Last week, Dave Reynolds from Channel 4 News in Oakland, California, was publicly beaten, hung during the six-o-clock news."

Morris shook his head. "Was he a Christian?"

"Yes, he was."

Their mentor was pensive for a moment. He recalled punishments of all faiths had ramped up since UNO's takeover. Lately, the Christian faith was being targeted a lot more. Joshua was confirming that revelation with details he was learning through his broadcasting endeavor. Benjamin considered their encounter months earlier at the library in the city a Godsend because of the confidential information on UNO he was uncovering. "So, what was the reason for this senseless beating?"

"Mr. Reynolds had been having secretive Bible gatherings at his house. UNO found out. The military seized him, drove him to the town square, and hung him. They made a mockery of him on television, just horrible."

Petra gasped and rubbed her dampened eyes. She hated hearing about the casualties around the country.

Caleb muttered something underneath his breath. *We have to be careful with our own meetings. What if they find us?*

Joshua snorted. "They aired this during the prime-time news hour, Dave's time slot just to make a point. He is survived by his wife and two-year-old son. It was an absolute blessing that his family wasn't home when it happened. We don't know where they are currently. I've reached out to a few dependable contacts in Los Angeles, they're looking for them."

Morris scribbled a few notes on the yellow pad. His leg suddenly cramped, and he got up, shaking it off. "Keep me updated on Mrs. Reynolds and her son if you hear anything. You know Christians have been persecuted for thousands of years. It hasn't stopped, either, only gotten worse. According to James 1:2, the verse tells us to count it all joy when we come into trials. This is a big trial we are facing. We must be diligent in our purpose, fighting for our faith, reaching people with the Bible so they can embrace salvation like us. Anything else?"

"No."

"Petra, what about you?"

The young woman hesitated. "—Give me a moment. This is very hard for me." Having been born in Ukraine before coming to the States, she witnessed many casualties perpetrated by the 2014

Russian and Ukrainian revolution. Even as a small child of four, she had watched the rising tensions between her home country and Russia before her family escaped in 2015. Since joining the team, after encountering Benjamin on campus at the University of Chicago during an Anthropology lecture, all she had been hearing about were these conflicts between UNO and Christians. It grieved her but she knew her skills would not go unnoticed. Her teacher assured her that her knowledge of languages and culture would come in handy one day. It was all it took to join.

"Take your time," Franklin said.

"—I'll go," blurted Caleb. "I have a question." Petra bowed her head, and their leader folded his arms. "Sure, speak up."

Caleb, feeling confident, sprang up from his chair. "I know our goal is tell people about Jesus, but I've also been hearing unsettling rumblings about the other religions. A friend of mine in Dearborn, Michigan sent me an encrypted message the other day about it. There have been multiple decapitations of Muslims who won't convert to KASTAM. It's mind-blowing. How did we get here without anyone *ever* stopping it?"

"I hear you," Benjamin remarked. He liked the young man and saw potential in him. *He's an eager warrior.* He had met Caleb the same day as Jacob, but at a coffee house. He was building a video game on his device. Impressed with his programming skills, organization, and coding, he approached him. He remembered thinking Caleb could be very useful in transcribing and delegating tasks.

Their leader continued, ambling in front of his stool. "When I was growing up there was always a rumor of a one-world government and one-dominating religion. The eradication of all history and faiths didn't happen overnight, either. It was a slow chipping away of freedoms replaced with immediate pleasures, which made us, the former American people, complacent. Many of you don't know the difference because you were born when things had been in the process of breaking down and the supposed 'new way' taking root. That is what UNO's laws and KASTAM have done. And this is what we are dealing with."

The candle flames shuddered at this somber truth, and each member went quiet, until Jacob's deck of cards slipped out of his grip and landed on the floor. "Oh, sorry," he mumbled as he scrambled to pick them up, remembering how he landed in the

United States at ten-years-old because of the rapid changes going on in his country.

Jacob's mother and father had him smuggled via a Canadian and American Freedom Trucking Convoy from Ottawa, Canada, over the border in 2022. He was raised by multiple families, lived in several parts of the States and regrettably, he never heard from his parents ever again.

Jacob survived by winning poker tournaments around the world. When Morris met him at a casino in Joliet, his teacher convinced him how vital a role he'd have on the team because he had traveled internationally and could gain access to government conventions held in London and Bern. *It's a long shot, but Morris has faith in me.*

The others scuffled their feet on the hardwood floor, Benjamin sensed fear and hesitancy within the bunch. Jacob riffle shuffled his cards, Joshua flexed his biceps, Caleb seemed jittery, Franklin tinkered with his hands in his pockets, and Petra wrote in her notebook. He turned to Petra, "Ready to fill us in?"

The only female representative of the crew arranged her notepad on her lap, recalling the beautiful family, recently torn up. "Okay. This wasn't brought to the forefront like Joshua's case, but I can tell you, it might have been. The small town of Dalton, Illinois, had been shaken. Irene Silverman's three-year-old twin girls were burned alive after UNO troops ambushed the town; a militant spotted Irene's cross-pendant dangling from her neck. They made her watch the brutal charring of her children as an example for others. I … I … my mother had known Irene's mom, that's how I got to meet this wonderful lady two years ago and learn about her devotion to God. We've kept in touch ever since. When I heard the news this past Monday, I was devastated." Petra took out a tissue and dabbed her eyes.

Jacob dropped his cards, jumped to his feet, and knelt beside Petra's chair, holding her in his arms as she sniffled.

"I'm sorry," Petra disengaged from the embrace and blew her nose. "Thank you, Jacob. It's just that I knew Irene's family. I've seen so much in my country, and now here too. We *told* her not to wear her cross pendant. Those babies would have lived."

Benjamin ran a hand down his face. "Judgment is coming for those who mock and hate Jesus Christ. Where is Irene now?"

"A friend's house. I don't know much about that family, but she's there. They told me Irene is not the same anymore."

Morris made another notation. "I'm sorry this happened. At least UNO didn't seize her or kill her too. Thank you, Petra."

Something clinked to the floor. Everyone turned.

Benjamin paused mid-step. "Franklin!" His pupil leapt up out of his chair, startled. He picked up the gadget that had slipped out of his pocket, a Timex watch with a stainless steel, two-toned expansion band that had belonged to his father, Deacon Don. *Why do I carry this thing still?* Embarrassed, he shook it, stuffed it in his pocket and said, "I'm so sorry, sir. It won't happen again. And Petra, I'm really sorry to hear about your friend. It is just terrible."

Their teacher sighed impatiently, "Go ahead."

Franklin shoved his hands in his pockets. "Ahh … I don't know how to follow up after hearing Petra's disturbing update."

She exhaled noisily, "It's okay, really."

The eldest warrior obliged. "Well, our satellite office in Buffalo, Wyoming, expanded its unit from twenty to thirty-three members in the past three weeks."

Petra clapped; the others nodded their heads in enthusiasm. Benjamin hiked back onto his chair. The cramping gone for the moment. "That's encouraging, Franklin. Is Dr. Lawrence running the camp?"

"Yes, they unearthed several old King James Bibles in the Cloud Peak Wilderness area hidden on Bomber Mountain."

"Why's it called 'Bomber Mountain'?" Caleb asked.

Franklin rubbed the watch in his pocket. "I asked that same question too. Dr. Lawrence said in 1943, during the Second World War, there was a plane carrying a crew of eleven American military soldiers, flying to Nebraska, and then to Germany to fight the Nazi's and Adolf Hitler. The plane crashed, the wreckage was discovered a couple of years later by two cowboys, but here's the ironic part."

Everyone leaned forward in their chairs.

"… The whole crew perished. Only one body was found, it was propped up against a rock, holding a wallet, family photos, and an open Bible lying next to him."

Petra gasped, "Oh, my! You don't think those old Bibles are from that wreckage?"

"No, those Bibles were found near there. There's no connection to the plane, but I'm intrigued about these vintage Bibles because they're on the same mountain as the plane with the one crew member who actually had a Bible in his hand before he died."

"Hmm … Divine Intervention," Morris commented.

Jacob, weaved shuffled his cards, while listening to this fascinating story, asked, "What are they going to do with the Bibles they've found?"

"Dr. Lawrence told me they are in a pretty fragile state with all the erosion and seasonal changes. They're going to figure out how old they are and try and reproduce them since most of the Bibles have been burned."

Benjamin agreed, "Good piece, Franklin. It would be great if those Bibles could be reprinted. In fact, Mark 16:14-20 and Matthew 28:16-20 mention the 'Great Commission'. Going out into the world and telling everyone, every human being about Jesus. This is why we're equipping ourselves to do for those who have never known Christ, and renewing the faith of those who have fallen away because of what KASTAM's indoctrination has done to their minds."

Franklin agreed, "I'm excited, even though there are troubles all around us. Biblical teaching is growing rapidly."

Benjamin puffed out his chest. "Yes, I'm also encouraged to hear from your reports that there are folks fighting for their faith in Jesus. I don't care about the other religions because there is only ONE. Jesus said in John 14:6: *'I am the way, the truth, and the life. No one comes to the Father except through Me.'* We're rekindlers remember, stirring up those who have been squashed, scared into fear, put under government submission and those who have lost their Christian faith. Our ministry requires effort, energy and perseverance from each of us."

The team lifted their fists and mouthed, "Oorah!" Morris saluted them. *God has this. No spirit of fear, Benji.* If UNO militants discovered him or any of his members, they would be killed right then and there. He'd already shared what he learned in the military: improvise, adapt, and overcome in case things changed.

Are these recruits willing to put their lives on the line for the good and glory of God? Time will tell. For now, he'd continue to pray over them.

Chapter 2 – The Brave and The Encourager

Something snapped and everyone spun around toward the kitchen. Morris stiffened, gesturing with his finger and falling to the floor. "Quiet!" The members followed suit. It was a safety measure their leader had been training them since they started gathering. He mouthed, "Someone, secure the grounds, immediately."

Joshua responded right away, "I'll go."

"Very well," Benjamin approved, feeling for the pistol in his ankle holster, just in case.

"I'll go with you," Caleb interjected.

"No way," Joshua stuttered, "this—this is a man's job, not a boy's."

Jacob tossed his cards in the air; Franklin and Petra glanced at him, snickering. Caleb inched forward. Morris shook his head, "Enough! Take care of the situation."

Joshua crawled into the kitchen. He'd show all of them what he was made of. *I'm not just a muscle guy.* Three years earlier his parents kicked him out of the house for not joining the UNO military. Homeless and starving on the streets of Los Angeles, he'd met some guys who were body builders. Instead of crumbling with pity, he threw himself into weight training and got in shape. He left California and came to Illinois to start over.

Using the knowledge he learned from his mother and father about UNO, Joshua landed a decent job at an online news outlet. He still had some self-esteem issues under those bulging biceps, for instance not understanding why his parents chose UNO over him, but thankfully, he was making efforts to redeem himself through Benjamin Morris' mentorship.

Carefully opening one of the kitchen drawers, Joshua pulled out a steak knife, rose to his feet, peeled back darkened shades, and peered through the window over the sink. He inched toward the backdoor, glancing back, making out the shadows of his party in the living room, their lives rested on his every move. Pivoting, he slowly turned the doorknob.

"Hey," Caleb whispered in his ear.

Joshua flinched, "Holy—"

Caleb covered Joshua's mouth, "Shh…" Chuckling, he realized the male model of the squad had finally been startled. *He's not so tough after all.*

"Don't ever do that again," Joshua stammered, trying to breathe and getting his adrenaline under control. "What are you doing here? I told you to stay behind."

"I came over because you'll need backup. Someone could have followed you know who," he motioned with his head toward Franklin; "he's so laid back."

Joshua tapped his chin with his finger. "You have a point." Even though he'd known Franklin for only half a year and heard all he'd done so far for their leader, he was still leery about Franklin. *Am I jealous of this guy because Morris looks to him for the 'big assignments,' or am I unsure about being able to hold my own?* Shaking off any other doubts, he said, "I'm going to open the door. We'll have to do this in the dark."

"Roger that."

"Once I see it's clear, I'll go left. You follow behind me and go right, got it?"

"Yep, easy-peasy," Caleb responded, thinking this would be no big deal. *Who can find us out here?* Noticing Joshua's knife, he scrunched up his face. "You think I'll need one of those, too?"

"… There," he pointed, "I got it out of that drawer, two down from the top drawer on the right."

As Caleb crept away, Joshua squinted at his peers talking softly. He could barely hear their voices. His attention diverted back to the youngest member, wielding two knives, one in each hand. "Dude, why do you need two?" Then, Joshua rolled his eyes, "Never mind, ready?"

"You're the boss, let's roll." Caleb said, roused to action.

Joshua put his sweaty hand on the knob, and slowly turned it as he straightened up. Opening the door, he pressed his head between the screen door and the door frame. *Rain, it smells like rain, AGAIN.* The gray-colored, brick bungalow-shaped house was surrounded by tall evergreens on all three sides. The backdoor adjoined a white-painted wooden porch. Three steps on either side led to a gravel path. On one side, the left side only, the porch steps connected to a gravel drive. The backyard's grass was overgrown with weeds. *How did Morris find this place?*

Earlier in the day, Benjamin had picked up everyone (where they were instructed to meet) at Union Station, and they drove over three hours on two-lane roads, avoiding the checkpoints on the highway. Parking the vehicle between trees and large bushes, they had hiked two-miles to this abandoned house.

Joshua shivered, feeling a cold dampness even though it was early May. *Darn climate change.*

Hearing nothing except the quick breathing of Caleb hovering over his shoulder, Joshua pushed the screen door open, sliding through, and motioning for the younger man to follow. "I'll go left, you go right. Circle your side of the house, turn around and meet me here on the porch. But before you circle back, look at your surroundings, take time to pay attention to any movement in the bushes or near the trees."

"Okay."

Joshua stepped onto the porch. It creaked, there was rotting, peeling wood in many spots. Caleb followed, turning right, as directed, he proceeded down the three steps to the side of the house, staying close to the brick wall. The dirt felt lumpy and uneven under his feet as he slinked across the wall, pausing now and then, glancing around as instructed. Coming close to a window ledge the young man tried to see inside, but the window shades were drawn tightly. *This house really does look like it's vacant.* Continuing on, he got to the front of the home and crouched near five brick steps that led to a front door. Gazing about, he saw nothing. There were no streetlights, just blackness. *No way I'd find this place in the dark, nor be able to leave. Luckily, Benjamin has planned for us to stay overnight.*

Caleb waited another minute or so, and then retreated back toward the porch. Joshua was already there, jamming his knife into the railing, and squinting out in the darkness. "See anything?"

"No. There's nothing out there."

"I'm glad. That sound could have been an animal, maybe a racoon."

Caleb suddenly felt silly holding his two knives. "Should we go in?"

The two men marched into the house. Caleb put the knives away while Joshua locked the door. All eyes turned on them once they regrouped in the living room.

Joshua looked at Morris, "So, we checked the perimeter and found nothing. It could have been a squirrel or another small animal."

Benjamin grinned in satisfaction. *Good. Glad it was nothing. We don't need to be discovered.* "Thank you. At ease, you both may be seated." His heart thumped erratically. *I have to tell them ...*

"I am being hunted for bringing people closer to Christ, and safety isn't always a guarantee."

"Absolutely, yes sir!" Franklin blurted.

Benjamin glared, "Do you?"

Franklin shrugged. "Of course, there is a huge risk in doing this kind of work. Look at the followers in Wyoming and how they've grown. We've got our jobs cut out for us, that's for sure." He winked at his mentor. "Don't forget we're learning from an experienced teacher, a great man."

Joshua and Caleb exchanged exasperated looks, and Jacob whispered, "Teacher's pet."

Morris was speechless. *Great is the farthest thing from my mind. Wanted for other reasons which I need to explain to this group very soon.* "Ahem ... I appreciate that, Franklin. Who's left to report? Jacob?"

"... Sir."

"You're up."

"Oh, right." Jacob put his cards down and leaned back in his chair. He didn't have any notes, nor was he ever prepared to speak, he hesitated. He'd rather be home. *Home? Where was that?* Right now, it was a room the size of a master bath at his cousin's house, third cousin by marriage. Playing competitive poker, he had been trying to save some money to get his own place, unfortunately he wasn't succeeding as quickly as he wanted. When Benjamin had approached him three months earlier at the Joliet Casino, the man's story gave Jacob a real purpose.

"Well, two weeks ago, the Nations of Unity, the NOU, had another election for a new council member—their second in eight months. Drago Cheztza is no longer with them. Rumor has it that he was a practicing Catholic, not an Atheist as he claimed when he joined the NOU. I think he was disposed of. A man named Arimus Popluouski has replaced him."

"What do we know about him?"

"Arimus is Greek by birth but has been living in London for the past seventeen-years. He did have a brief residency in Turkey. He is fifty-four-years-old and has never been married. Rumor is, he's a big deal maker, good friends with President Philip Borsta II. Hmm, no coincidences here. And, Mr. Popluouski has an appetite for young, dark-haired middle-eastern women."

"Pervert," Joshua snorted, disgusted by the background of the NOU council member.

Jacob glanced over at Joshua in agreement. "I'm going to keep an eye on this one. He's a big supporter of KASTAM. I've got a poker tournament coming up next month in London, and if you don't mind, I'd like to stay a bit and investigate Arimus' motives."

"Why certainly Jacob, that's a great idea." Morris pointed at Petra, "You might want to partner up with her. Don't you know Greek?"

"Yes, enough to get by."

Standing up and taking a couple steps toward the heavily-draped front window, Benjamin turned and leaned on the windowsill ledge. "Then it's settled. Work it out among yourselves and make plans, figure out how both of you are going."

Jacob pumped a fist in the air. "Yes, this could work. Most of the governmental officials gamble. I could use Petra's skills to spy on them."

Petra put her hand over her heart. "Thank you, Captain, for this."

"—Wait!" Caleb blurted. "Won't it be too dangerous for Petra to go to London, she's the only girl here."

"He's not wrong," Joshua replied.

Jacob sputtered. "Don't you think I know that? I've been taking care of myself. You think I can't watch out for Petra too?"

Petra waved her arms. "Um … Hello. I'm right here, boys. You could talk directly to me. I come from Ukraine; I've seen some terrible things. I can take care of myself, too."

Franklin interrupted. "—She's right. I trust Petra will be fine."

"Thank you," Petra responded. *At least someone thinks I can stand on my own two feet.*

Embarrassed, Caleb remarked, "I didn't mean you were weak, Petra. You know, it's just—" *You remind me of the older sister I never had the opportunity to meet.*

She waved her hands, dismissing the incident. "I understand. Thank you for looking out for me. Don't worry, okay?"

Benjamin grinned. It was apparent to him that in the little time the group had been together, they were starting to look out for one another. This pleased him and he was thankful to the Lord for directing him to find these five specific disciples and assembling this new team. *I know, Lord, your timing is not my timing.*

Morris had befriended each of the members within a six-month time period after a long two-year hiatus. During that time, the former Marine studied the Scriptures and strategized ways to reach people with the Good News, while searching for new recruits. His biggest challenge over the past twenty years was not being discovered while recruiting individuals to join this evangelistic calling. Many of his past pupils left, fearful for their lives, and some tragically died. It was always a risky undertaking.

This was his seventh taskforce after six failed startups. Benjamin's new squad was different. Their minds were open, they exhibited a curiosity to God's Word. They were also educated on the current rules, laws and KASTAM, without being indoctrinated. God had selected each of these individuals just for him.

"Then it's settled. Let's move on. Who's left?"

Caleb sprung to his feet and drew out an index card from his back pocket. "I am." Christianity was a whole new religion for him. Growing up on the south side of Chicago, his parents never talked about religion. He knew now that they had been fearful of what the UNO military would do, it was KASTAM or nothing. His Grandpa Phil told him he used to be a Catholic many years before his birth, and practiced his faith until Caleb's older sister, Magdalene, had passed, and then he'd stopped altogether.

Magdalene had a rare disease and died when she was nine-months-old. Caleb had never met her, born three years later. His family had made it a point not to discuss her death.

Caleb's grandfather, now deceased for eight years, had also tried sharing some tidbits on Christian principles, but his mother had interceded and halted the conversation. Through Benjamin's teachings, he was learning so much about God and Jesus that he wanted to have an impact in the world.

Morris gestured with his arm. "Proceed."

"Um, on the North Shore, two mosques have been burned down, killing twenty-five civilians. We don't know who did this, but my best guess, if I may …"

The others grumbled, Caleb stared back at them, not sure what that meant. "… Captain?"

Benjamin pulled away from the ledge and chuckled. From the other member's mutterings, he had a feeling an initiation of some kind would come soon, and that Franklin would oversee it.

Clearing his throat, their leader commented, "Stop whining. Give the man an opportunity to speak. One thing I want you to get clear Caleb is that you, as well as the others here, are my connection to what's happening in the world. You're my troops on the ground, whether it be the suburbs, the city, or anywhere else around the world. I expect you to add your speculations, comments, recommendations, because you are hearing and seeing things firsthand. Don't be afraid to speak up. Everyone copy that?"

The rest of the group mumbled a 'yes'; Caleb looked relieved. Benjamin could relate to the youngest disciple. *He is trying at least.* He had enthusiasm and perseverance, but he also desired respect from his peers. *A lot like me and even better prepared to succeed.*

Benjamin Morris was born to Italian and Irish parents who immigrated to the States. His father, Earl, was a mail carrier for the Post Office, and his mother, Claire, was a cook at their neighborhood elementary school. Neither Earl nor Claire was remotely religious, even when all faiths in the USA were tolerated, but they were strict and pushed him to do better. Sadly, everything Morris tried to do well, whether in school, work, or even in his military experience, he was always passed over when up for promotion but never daunted by it.

Their leader twisted his hands. "Continue."

"Oh, yes, right." Caleb fidgeted with the index card, feeling self-conscious all of a sudden. He had never been treated with dignity by anyone, not even his parents, who seemed to have sheltered him from his faith and world knowledge. He was gaining so much more with this new group.

"Um … I suspect these mosque burnings are being done by an anti-government organization. I'm waiting for confirmation on that. I've also heard in recent weeks about an underground Christian organization making waves. I'm still investigating this too. Maybe we can partner up with these folks?"

Benjamin held up his hand. "Great Caleb, but let's not join forces with these individuals just yet. We need to be careful. There are a few out there, but not enough to know exactly what they stand for and what they are doing. Our intention is to revive Christianity, not burn temples and mosques. And the burnings concern me. If that's the case we are fighting KASTAM the same way they are trying to beat us."

Caleb's shoulders sagged. He thought that joining another troop would help them grow. Petra stopped writing and looked from her leader to Caleb. Everyone else went silent.

Morris regarded Caleb's frown, and spoke again, "Eyeballs on me."

Caleb raised his eyes, fearful of what was to come next.

"I'm not reprimanding you. I have two decades of experience organizing teams. Firstly, we need to grow organically ourselves. Secondly, our intention involves *no violence*. Do I make myself *crystal* clear?"

Caleb acknowledged his teacher and sat down. "Yes, Captain." Pulling out a pen, he made a notation on his card. He'd try harder to get things straight, learning all that he could.

Chapter 3 – The Enlightenment

Morris checked his watch. It was just a little past 2100 hours. The summaries from each member had taken a little over an hour, including the time it took for Joshua and Caleb to surveil the property. This was their eighth in-person meeting, and with all their discussions and experiences, he was beginning to recognize each of the members unique talents.

Benjamin moved away from the window and lumbered back to his barstool, picking up a tan briefcase from the floor. The contents would finally be shared this evening. A few minutes went by as he rummaged through it. The members spoke to one another in whispers, anticipating their teacher's next steps.

I need to think about how to best present this. Come on, get your bearings. "Attention everyone, take a break. There's food and drink in the icebox. Grab some chow, let's come back at 2130 hours."

The members jumped to their feet at the chance for a snack. Franklin and Joshua bolted to the bathroom, but Franklin beat him to it, sliding through the door, mocking his colleague and flexing his muscles.

"Screw you, meathead," Joshua growled, slamming his fist on the door.

"Cut it out," Benjamin called from the living room, "be civil. You're lucky I have good connections, or you'd all go hungry tonight and we'd be sleeping under the stars."

"Sorry," Joshua murmured, falling back against the door just as Petra, Caleb, and Jacob walked past him, sneering.

Entering a bare kitchen from the hallway, Jacob turned on a small lamp that barely illuminated the room. In the center was a round table with four wobbly chairs. Along the wall under a square window was a stainless-steel sink with a white Formica countertop. Another door led to the backyard, the same one Joshua and Caleb had secured. He trotted over and shook the doorknob.

"We locked it already," Caleb scolded.

"Hmm, I can see that," Jacob replied over his shoulder. *I'm ensuring our safety. We've moved so much, I never know.*

Caleb opened the refrigerator. "Brussel sprouts, canned peas, hummus, cranberry jelly, you call this food? I can't eat this stuff." He looked in the cupboard, "Prune juice, cod liver oil? Yuck, where's the carbonated water?"

Petra was bellied over the table, giggling. Additional food items were under the sink. She bent down to open the cabinet. Caleb turned, "What are you doing?"

Petra motioned him toward her, "Let me show you the real food." Inside a miniature-sized icebox were lunchmeats of all kinds, bread, yogurt, soft drinks, water bottles, prepared salads, and other items. "Now this is what I'm talking about," Caleb dove in, pulling out various items and placing them on the table.

Jacob joined him and together they made sandwiches. Petra grabbed a bottle of water and removed a can of nuts from one of the cupboards. She munched, watching the guys when Franklin and Joshua swaggered in.

Franklin gave Petra a big smile. "What are you eating?"

"Nuts."

"Nuts, huh, sounds good, but I need something more sustaining than that." Franklin licked his lips at the double-decker sandwich Caleb and Jacob had finished fixing. "Caleb, can you make me one of those?"

"… Coming right up."

Joshua circled the kitchen, futzing with the window shades he previously examined during his perimeter check. *All is quiet.*

"Joshua, you want a sandwich too?"

"Sure, whatever you're having." He fell into one of the wobbly chairs at the end of the table. The others ate in silence relishing the time away from Morris' rigorous teachings. Petra, however, snuck peaks at their leader; she was ready to go again.

Hovering over the barstool, Benjamin fingered the pages in his hands. They were old and yellowed with age. *How do I share this with my squad? I know You want me to do this. You've been nudging me to present this to them, this team in particular. I don't know how I feel about revealing it, but I must be obedient to You, Lord.* He glanced at his watch—2127 hours. *Time for a quick bathroom break.*

Franklin placed his trash in the garbage and saw Morris standing. "Come on. He doesn't like us to be late."

The others followed the eldest and cleared away their food scraps. As the pupils filed back into the living room, Benjamin hobbled ahead. Petra noticed he was favoring his good leg a bit more. "How are you doing with that today, sir?"

Their leader turned. "Some days are better than others." Arriving at his seat, Morris gritted his teeth and sat down. Long ago memories invaded his thoughts. Twenty-four years earlier, he was an American citizen, a father, and a captain in the Marines. Now, he was without heritage and culture, or citizenship. Everything he knew about this country, principles and spirit, wiped away, out of sight and mind. *I used to brew in hate and live in despair. All that changed with my encounter with Jesus. There was a better way of resolving the wickedness of the world. I'm going to try and restore things for this country.*

Joshua coughed and Benjamin looked up, clearing his throat, "I apologize, where was I?"

Caleb answered, "… I don't know. Are you going to give us an assignment?"

Morris shook his head. "… Not yet."

The candle to Morris' right was snuffed out by a light breeze, the wick bent into the small pool of liquid wax. Smoke swirled up into the air. "Put your books away. I have a story to tell you."

Benjamin relit the extinguished candle with the flick of a match. He scrutinized each of his pupils. Trepidation had suddenly clouded his senses; he was unsure of his pupils' reactions to the sharing of the letter. *I've carried these yellow, frail pages with me for an awfully long time, never sharing them with anybody, not even my previous groups. Alright God, I don't know what reaction I'm going to get, but I'm going to trust You with this.* He gingerly held up several pages. "Do you know what I have here?"

Caleb narrowed his eyes. "Ah, they look like a bunch of old papers?" Everyone else laughed.

"These pages have seen some mileage that's for sure," Morris agreed. "This is a piece of history you'll never get from any of your devices."

Franklin, suddenly sat up, "What are they about?"

A little tease might work here. "Are you interested?" The team had shifted to full attention. Benjamin ran his fingers along the edges of the pages, having read the letter many times over, and visualizing the emotion of the writer.

He gazed intently at his warriors. "I have a married daughter who lives in the city. We're not on the best of terms. I have a four-year-old grandson named Frederick. I see him from time to time. Not too long ago he showed me a backpack he dug up at a park nearby. Frederick loves digging in dirt and grass." Benjamin grinned in adoration. "I'll never understand kids and their love of dirt."

Most of the members smiled at their leader's affection for his grandson. Franklin huffed instead, "You went into the city? That's dangerous! What if you were caught?" *He preaches to us about safety, but yet he visits his family in the open.*

Petra glared at Franklin. "Excuse me, don't talk to him that way."

Benjamin cleared his throat. "He's right. I'm always reminding all of you to be careful. It was dangerous and very risky, yes." Everyone gave a thumbs up except Franklin who still felt miffed by this visitation.

"Inside the backpack were these pages. A letter depicting the last days of our beloved United States before it became UNO."

Petra shrieked, "Wow! What?"

Franklin gulped, not knowing what to make of this new revelation. Both Jacob and Joshua looked at each other in amazement.

"Oh, man." Caleb muttered.

Jacob burst out, "—Are you going to tell us about this letter?"

Morris stood up. "With your permission, I'd like to read these pages to you. It will give you a perspective on our history."

Petra clapped, "Yes, yes, please!"

He grinded his teeth. "Argh ..." his leg shook under the duress of the stinging daggers shooting down his calf. Benjamin twitched about, sliding off and then hiking back onto the stool again. "Alright, here it is." His watch read 2145 hours.

June 6, 2008

If you found this you can safely assume I have been captured by UNO, or I'm dead.

I'm a Christian but I have lived among Muslims, Hindus, Jews, and Non-believers. My story is not unique. I am a simple man in my late thirties. I've had many regrets and lost a lot in my life. They, the conspiracy theorists, said it was coming—the end of the United States. It was all over social media. Nobody would believe it because the government was categorizing it as misinformation. I believed it and it happened. In these final days I know it is my duty to tell you what really happened. The media wants you to believe this is a peaceful collaboration of all countries to unify the economy and religion. What actually occurred was not that at all. The predestined date would be June tenth. Four days from now.

However, everything is in chaos. Grocery stores have been stripped and robbed clean. Vandalism and murder is everywhere. Desperation prowls the streets.

I had a good job, cars, and money to spend on entertainment. I took my God-given freedoms for granted because I'm homeless now, somewhere in downtown Chicago, far from Evanston. All the streets look the same, I'm floundering. My wife kicked me out for my beliefs in Christ because I knew things were changing in the world and I desired to get right with God. My two teen daughters won't talk to me.

I became a Jesus follower. He was a "fisher of men." Losing my worldly life was worth it. I heard a preacher once say, 'Being a Christian won't cost you anything, it will cost you everything.' I wasn't going to conform to this wicked new regime. I sit in an alleyway hiding, unclean, whiskered, starving. UNO's military is coming. If you don't join, you die.

Morris stopped and turned the page. His stomach churned. *No matter how many times I've read this story, I always get this sickening feeling in the pit of my belly.* Looking around at his warriors, he wondered what each was thinking.

Joshua, intrigued by this mystery man, was grateful for the pause in this reading. He had so many questions to ask. He sat straighter in his chair; aware his shoulders had been hiked up in concentration. He raised his hand.

Benjamin nodded. "Speak up. What's on your mind?" The squad stared at Joshua.

"What's his name?"

Franklin shifted in his seat, annoyed. "Does the name matter? The guy wanted to put on paper the last days, you moron."

"I know that, but I'm still wrestling with why him. How come there aren't more of these…these diaries, written pages from the last days. I mean," Joshua motioned to their leader, "you were part of it. Where's your diary of this event?"

Morris tensed. *My life story is plagued with evil. I'm not proud of it.*

Jacob, bothered by Joshua's interrogation, interceded. "We're here, right? Aren't his efforts enough to convince you? You need proof?"

Joshua squeezed his fists and glared at their teacher suspiciously.

Benjamin put down the papers and removed his sweater. *Whoa, it's getting hot.* Closing his eyes, he couldn't help recalling the flashes of Afghanistan's desert terrain. He was in a trench with three other combat soldiers. The air was thick and heavy. The skyline looked like dirty cheese curds floating in the atmosphere. Every breath Morris took, he inhaled fumes, ash, the pungent smell of burning flesh. It felt like ninety-eight-degrees. Every few minutes there was a display of fireworks and fireballs falling from the sky, men calling out orders and there was screaming, but Benjamin couldn't make out what they were saying. He was sweating profusely, trying to stay alive all the while concerned about the terror happening thousands of miles away on American soil. The recollection quickly faded. He folded his sweater and fixed his polo shirt in his belted pants.

Franklin, reclining in his chair, interrupted his leader's ritual. "Well?"

Morris snapped back, "What?" Petra stopped her doodling.

"Where were you when 'it' happened?"

Benjamin exhaled and raised his arms toward the ceiling. "Oh God, everyday I've asked for your forgiveness for the events of June 2008. You've given me the pain in my leg as a reminder of my penance to you, and the purpose of my new life to revive Your Word and make You known."

Caleb cracked his knuckles—*Why is Morris acting so weird?* Their teacher faced them. "You know how I've told you a little about my Marine days. In late May of 2008, I was the captain of a combat unit. We were stationed in Texas at Fort Hood. My superior, Lt. Col. Howard Rohls, had requested six comrades, including myself into his office. Rohls had received classified intelligence about a potential military take-over on U.S. soil, occurring the first week of June."

Benjamin recalled how his other colleagues wanted to get involved right away and fight, but he wanted nothing to do with America anymore. It had taken him almost four years just to get to his position in the military and he was furious having to wait so long. *I'm a coward.* His marriage was also on the brink of destruction, and when he caught his wife cheating, it solidified the decision to leave. He shook his head. "Almost a thousand soldiers were already in Afghanistan, fighting a smaller scale war over oil."

He plodded to the window ledge, leaning against it, "I was the only one wanting to go to Afghanistan. I was deployed on the thirtieth of May and the attacks began on June fifth."

Morris coughed. "On that fifth of June, several bombs exploded on Fort Hood, killing many soldiers. My Lieutenant Colonel was killed and most of my platoon were seriously injured." He hung his head low. "I had abandoned them. I should have stayed. I hate myself for deserting my country."

Joshua closed his eyes. *Wow. What a story.*

No one else spoke for a time. The air smelled of burning wax. Finally, Jacob said, "What could you have done differently, Captain? It sounds like it was already in the works."

Benjamin sighed. … *Died alongside my fellow marines.*

"We support you," the others replied, and Petra wiped a tear heading down her cheek. *I've never seen him like this.*

Morris carefully arranged the yellowed sheets again. "Ahem, okay. Anyhow, the man's name in the letter is Dennis. Shall I read some more about him?"

All chimed in, "Yeah, sure, yes."

June 7, 2008

I'm still alive God. Thank you for another night. The rumble woke me, ten stretch vehicles and several buses were making their way south on Michigan Avenue. Four men dressed in military garb jump off vehicles and dart between buildings. I wasn't going to wait to meet my destiny with these masked gorillas. Gathered backpack, headed west. Didn't get far, my feet throbbing. Stopped in doorway took off my shoes, socks shredded. Blisters on bottom of soles. Wiped puss off. Had to keep going, took a deep breath, slipping my shoes back on, treading through alleyways away from Michigan Avenue, frequently looking back for any militia.

I'm starving. Saw three vehicles drive east of me. I hear screaming, civilians captured. Baseball dugout my only shelter, flashlight is flickering. Eyeing meager supplies, some water and three tiny candy bars. I pray for a safe evening.

Morris let the last sentence linger in the dim-lit room for a bit longer ... *Pray for a safe evening. This is what I do every single time we meet.* Worried faces greeted his own. *I hope they realize time was running out for Dennis.* The final days were upon him; there was nothing anyone in that room could have done to change the course of events which led them to the here and now.

Franklin played with his watch's expansion band. He pictured Dennis as a scrawny man, shivering in a school's baseball dugout, cold, and hungry, wanting so much to survive the night, and the flickering flashlight, with its batteries running out were symbolic of the destiny that would soon end his life. *Batteries? How ironic that I'm thinking about them. Why am I thinking about batteries?*

Franklin squeezed the gadget in his hand so tight his fingers started turning blue. *I should just throw this thing out the window.* Regrettably, it was the only reminder of his father, a revered deacon from their Catholic church in Lexington, Kentucky, where he grew up. His father was removed from his role as a deacon when allegations of him sexually molesting altar servers surfaced. The last child, a boy around twelve years of age, was found hiding in the Sacristy's bathroom holding batteries to a dimming flashlight. Franklin was the one who had found him.

For a long time, Franklin couldn't look at a flashlight or a battery because of the incident and the trauma that ensued on his family and the congregation. His mother divorced his father and they moved to another part of Lexington. He was four-years-old at the time and the state-wide takeover by UNO had commenced.

Leaving his dad was difficult. Franklin loved him so much. He never understood why they left; he was angry with his mother for a long time. They stopped practicing their Catholic faith too. When he was eleven, his mom explained the truth about his father and the altar servers and for years thereafter, it messed with his psyche. *That flickering flashlight!*

Franklin abruptly rose from his seat, marched to the corner of the room and threw the watch in the trash can. *I need to move on right here and now.* It made a loud thud against the metal cylinder. Sitting down, he put his hands to his face and started praying.

Joshua mouthed to Caleb, *what in the world?*

Petra crossed and uncrossed her legs. She felt anxious for him. *That was strange, poor Franklin. He must be really worried about Dennis' life. I feel the same way.*

"—Are you okay?" Benjamin asked.

Franklin lifted up his head. "I am now." *It's over. I'm not going to think about my father anymore. I'm a new creation in Jesus. It's about time I let all this go.*

Petra looked around. "So, are you going to finish the rest of the story tonight?"

Morris didn't know what tomorrow would bring but redemption was at hand. He glanced at his watch, 2205 hours. *Tomorrow is less than two hours away. I should finish this story and ...* He nodded, "affirmative."

Jacob gave a thumbs-up. "Woo-hoo!"

Caleb's mind spun in circles. "Wait. I'm curious. Who are these militia bandits Dennis is referring to?"

"Good question. Let me break it down for you. In 2008 President Alan J. Broadview was assassinated by a hired hitman who worked for a rich business mogul, Kirby Borsta. At the time, Mr. Borsta was head of the World Elite Committee or WEC. This organization was comprised of billionaire partners and their companies. Their goal: shape the global, regional, and industrial agendas and become the decision-makers for the entire world. Kirby became President and World Leader, and his sons were employed via WEC. It was Kirby Borsta who dismantled the USA and the rest of the world. He and his militia were taking over the US, one state at a time. Their goal was to achieve full control by June tenth. We now know they accomplished this. So, Caleb, these bandits are UNO militia, and Dennis appears to be writing this experience that happened in downtown Chicago."

Joshua scratched his chin. "Isn't President Philip Borsta II Kirby's son?"

"Yes."

Caleb shook his head. "Geez, no nepotism there."

Petra raised her hand. "It's incredible how you've come from such a different background than us with different presidents and different religions, while we've been born into this one-world government and one-religion."

Morris concurred. "Not to mention the erasing of the Church, replaced with the religion of electronics, technology, virtual reality, and instructions on how to remain 'functional' in society, all compacted into your Visphonice booklet you all are expected to carry at all times." Their teacher paused, turned, and from his carrycase, pulled out KASTAM's religious content for emphasis, a hundred-page, blood-red hardcover booklet. "I know you have your copy with you."

"Uh, huh," the teammates groaned in unison.

Benjamin smiled. "UNO controls food, money, transportation, and medical relief, as well as tracking everything you do. It was prophesied in Revelations 13 ... *'and that no one may buy or sell except one who has the mark of the beast, or number of his name.'* You understand now why I had you go through that rough 'cleansing' process when we commenced because of *their* technology in our bodies. Continue to be extremely careful. I'll assume you're all following the diet and taking the vitamins I've given you."

"Yes, Captain!"

Benjamin sat down and rubbed his bad leg. Retrieving his clipboard, he scanned his scribbles. *Phew ... this was a lot to go over with this letter. God, I pray through this story revelation these soldiers comprehend the importance of their role within this group and glorify You.* "Give me a few minutes. I have to check some things."

Back in the kitchen with his colleagues, Caleb paced back and forth in front of the backdoor. Petra looked his way, "What's going on?"

Caleb stared into Petra's green eyes. *Why is she even here? Things aren't safe.* He took a deep breath, "I'm starting to get a little scared. I mean, we are doing something really dangerous, this evangelizing ministry. We are the minority—Christians."

Franklin snorted between sips of Cola. "Getting cold feet, Caleb?"

Jacob flicked a six of spades at the youngest. "Ooh … I can feel the chill in the air."

Joshua laughed. He knew Caleb might freak out at some point. "You're not going to desert us, are you, baby?"

"Get over yourself, Joshua," Caleb growled. *Who is he to judge me anyway?*

"Stop it, boys," Petra blatted. She grabbed a can of soda and scooted next to Franklin. "Isn't there a scripture lesson here, something Jesus said … there aren't many laborers, but the harvest is plenty?"

"—Luke something, or maybe Mathew something," cut in Jacob.

Joshua shook his head. "No, I just read it the other day. It's Luke 10:2."

"Whatever." Caleb grimaced, going to the kitchen sink, running the faucet and vigorously scrubbing his hands. *They don't understand.* Ripping a piece of paper towel, he turned around.

Franklin drained the last of his soda and crushed the can. "Relax, will you. We're all part of this greater purpose of evangelizing. It's risky, yes, what we're doing. But you've got to believe God will protect us in our efforts. Reread Psalm 91. It's pretty clear that God will deliver you from your enemies, and you can take refuge under His wing or something like that. Get into the Word, brother."

Caleb collapsed in the chair across from Franklin, fatigue wearing down his mental state with the evening's information overload. "I get it," he uttered, "but I still can't help feeling insecure about how we can make a tremendous change."

Franklin nodded, relating to Caleb's apprehension. He felt the same in the beginning too. "Where's your faith? Believe me, you can, I can, she can," he said, pointing to his peers. "We just got to trust each other…and Morris too. We will grow organically like he said, and eventually they'll be more of us than them."

Petra sighed. "He's right. We have to continue to study the Scriptures, recruit people and grow. I'm sick of this KASTAM!"

Jacob smiled, "Amen! I'm with ya."

"Let's regroup." Benjamin called. Franklin got up and tossed his can in the trash. The others cleaned up and filed out of the kitchen.

Morris cracked his knuckles. "We're going to finish Dennis' story and discuss a few things. Your rooms are ready upstairs. We'll get some shut-eye and leave here at 0700 hours, any questions?"

Petra shrugged, Franklin sucked on his pen, Joshua stretched his arms overhead, Jacob snapped his fingers approvingly, and Caleb didn't respond, instead he focused on his feet.

Benjamin said, "Very well." He put down his clipboard and picked up Dennis' sheets again.

Chapter 4 – The Tale of Stories

June 8, 2008

My arms and legs are stiff, hard bench. The air cloudy, like big dust balls floating around. I peer across the field, no movement. I am hungry. I have a tiny candy bar and maybe a cup of water left. Need to find more to eat, won't survive much longer.

Consuming the last of my food, I climb out of the dugout. After several blocks sneaking and crawling between buildings, I see a dark brownstone. The front door is slightly ajar. Hearing nothing inside, I climb a flight of stairs to an apartment door and try turning the knob. It's locked. I knock softly, no answer. I trudge up another flight of stairs, side-stepping human feces and garbage, smell is putrid. At the next apartment, I put my hand on the doorknob. This time, it turns. A pair of hairy arms grab me and throw me to the floor. A shotgun digs into my neck.

Holding hands up, I croak, "Stop! I'm not one of them." A man, mid-forties, unshaven, smelling of sour lunchmeat, removes gun from my face, helping me up. A woman and two young children, a girl and boy, emerge from a dark hallway.

I learn they're hiding out, hoping to be lucky. We spend the next hour discussing our situation and how we might survive. It's a strained conversation, the man speaks mostly Spanish and broken English.

Marco, his name. Has a radio, on every channel, news about the takeover. Citizens are being hunted down and captured but verbal reports are contrary. We are isolated, with no news from other states.

And, stupid me, I'm still downtown. I've been so disoriented that I've made one big circle. I'm not familiar with city streets.

In a brief time, I somehow have become part of this family, and am given a can of warm beer and a hard piece of pita bread stuffed with a few lima beans. It's the most I've eaten in days.

I am urged to stay in the apartment above. The last tenant was captured by militia. The small children cry constantly, my nerves are a jangled mess.

Should I stay or leave now? Marco is friendly, but I don't feel safe, I fear the militia may come back, and we'll all be taken. I stay for the night. I will have to leave before sunrise; I must keep moving.

Morris folded the letter on his lap and paused. "What are your thoughts about what Dennis is going to do?"

Franklin spat out his gum into a tissue. "He has got to keep moving, survival, plain and simple."

Petra shook her head, "What about that family? He can't leave them."

Jacob played with his cards, doing an overhand shuffle, while Joshua jumped in, "Dennis has to leave. He knows it's only a matter of time before that family is captured. Marco can't go anywhere, not with two small kids. I also know how the communication is being disseminated. This government has the ability to change the narrative and shut off information at a press of a button."

"How depressing," Petra commented.

Benjamin shook his head, "Yes, it is. Unfortunately, if Dennis can't mobilize, things might be dire for him."

Caleb tried placing himself in Dennis' position. "What's worse is that he's downtown. He doesn't even know exactly where he is or where he's going. I'd be doing the same thing—preparing to leave at first light."

"I get the feeling the streets are not deserted either; civilians are in hiding," Petra said.

Morris agreed. "Yes. There is a massive militia presence, and they are going street by street seizing them. They know the territory, and the population, they've researched the downtown area. This was a well-thought-out plan. They'll get them and that family."

"You're right, that's what I was thinking," Jacob responded.

"Only two more days left before the *big* takeover. June tenth, right?" Franklin said.

"Correct." Benjamin stood and stretched his arms at his sides. Gingerly walking to the window, uneasiness momentarily gripped him, he felt a drop of cold sweat go down his spine. *We are safe. We checked the perimeter. Shake it off. God is with us.* He hastily limped back to his barstool.

Jacob stared at his leader's change in demeanor. *Is he okay?* He looked around at his colleagues and they didn't notice or seem concerned. For a time, all was still until Morris broke the silence with his heavy boots, as he settled back down on his seat. "Let's continue."

June 9, 2008

Before I slip out, I kneel near a crucifix and pray for this family's safety even though I know they don't stand a chance. Hoisting my backpack, I pull out a tarnished pocketknife and place it on the counter, my only 'thank you' for their hospitality.

Outside, a light wind blows through my t-shirt. I spy a tanker coming from my left. Throwing myself against doorframe, body shaking. A door slams and children crying—Marco's family knows. The family is doomed. My indecisiveness lasts a few moments. Another tanker is rounding the corner. I turn and run, heading toward Lake Michigan. I run for blocks, deeper into the city, it's the wrong way.

Many people, hundreds, run toward the lake. I pass alleyways, seeing other tankers roaring down streets. My God, there is no place to go. I push myself to run faster. My feet are on fire, in so much pain.

Stopping, out of breath, two burly men barrel over me, I'm shoved to the ground. When I get up, I find myself leaning against an old Amoco Oil building. The "o" at the end of Amoco is no longer readable, spelling "Amoc". I only see the word, Amok.

My wife, my daughters, my dog, my job, my friends, and everything that has ever defined my life bolted through my mind like lightning. I weep, watching more people scrambling past me, frenzied by their impending fate. I clutch my backpack—everything I've felt and experienced is in this bag. The truth will come out. I run.

The smell of boiled eggs lets me know I am getting closer to my destination, but the sounds of the tankers are also getting closer. Seeing Columbus Drive and Lake Shore Drive, I weave into Grant Park. Doors open and close; running boots can be heard on the lawn. I enter a small clearing and begin digging. I hurry. I need a hole big enough to hide my backpack. Satisfied, I grab my bag, stuff it in the hole, quickly covering it up.

I leap up and sprint toward Lake Shore Drive until I feel a thick rope around my neck.

Morris delicately folded the pages and waited for commentary.

Joshua spoke, "Hold up. Your grandson found this backpack in Grant Park? Why didn't you tell us earlier?"

"I knew it would be revealed, so why spoil it."

"That's smart." Franklin commented.

Petra, shocked by the details of the letter, clutched her midsection as a cramp surged through her body. She muttered, "I … I don't like this. Grabbed like a dog with a rope around one's neck seemed so—"

Jacob sat up, "Barbaric!

"Yes! Something is not right."

Morris grinned, "Petra, please explain further."

"For one, if Dennis buries his letter, wipes his hands, runs, and then gets captured, how does he know that's how he gets caught?"

Caleb and Jacob agreed. "—Good question."

Joshua pointed to their teacher. "What's your conclusion?"

Benjamin rubbed his chin. "Dennis was captured, and then he went back to finish the letter."

Caleb shook his head. "That can't possibly be true. He went back just to add that last sentence. Come on ..." The others laughed it off.

Morris held Caleb's gaze. "I have the sheets in my hand, the last sentence of that page is written in blue ink. The other pages are written in black."

"You're sure about this? Let me see." Petra said, taking the pages from her leader. "Oh, he's right! They are a different color, but the handwriting is the same."

"Gee, I look at Dennis differently now. I had respect for him, but now I don't think so," Franklin grunted.

Benjamin lifted himself up from his chair. "Let's not rag on the man. I think he wanted to leave something behind, his truth. This is a real piece of historical truth, what actually happened, not what we were told about a smooth transition into a one-world government and one-world religion."

"It's still not fair," Petra huffed, folding her arms, and sitting down again. Her heart had gone out to this man. "What if he became part of the militia? Or did he die?"

Morris observed his team, their faces were somber, confused, and they seemed disappointed. "Think logically for a minute." he trudged over to the front window again, settling on the ledge. "I bet you feel you've been on a wild goose chase?"

"Yeah uh, huh," everyone replied one after the other.

Benjamin puffed out his chest. "Alright, I have read and reread the letter more than a hundred times. What he experienced was painful. Imagine how the city looked, deserted, looted, and no one was willing to help. Cities and towns one by one were being disseminated and trashed. This takeover changed America. Now, picture a lonely man who has lost everything, his family, job, what is left of him and his dignity. He knew he would either be captured or perish. On the run, apparently running in circles, because he never even got out of the city. But who knows if he had gone farther out, the other way, if he would have been safer?"

Joshua shrugged, "I still don't know why Dennis would want to go back and add the last sentence to his letter, or if he did at all for that matter."

Caleb slapped his fist on his leg. "What a waste of a read!"

Benjamin ogled him. "—Got another conclusion?"

Petra couldn't visualize any other scenario for Dennis except what her leader offered. "There must be more to this story. Are there other pages?"

Here we go. Morris snapped his fingers and bent down to pick up his briefcase when the back door was kicked open, the window above the sink shattered, and the kitchen table tumbled over.

"What in the—" Benjamin barked.

Chapter 5 – The Raid and The Fugitive

The candles toppled over to the floor and the room filled with smoke. Shadows moved; it was impossible to see faces. The air smelled of burning wicks, extinguished fire, and sweat. Petra's arms were pulled roughly behind her back and tied together with cords around her chair, and a dirty cloth was stuffed in her mouth.

"What's happening?" Caleb cried out, as his body was slammed to the floor, a knife pressing into his neck.

Morris, now in a chokehold, wheezed for air. "Shut your mouth!" a tall male with a British accent bellowed.

Franklin, wrestled to the ground, struggled to get up, but his captor was much bigger and stronger than him. Jacob's cards were ripped out of his hands as he was pitched against the wall.

Joshua, bound like Petra, was the only one able to make out the abductors amidst the cloudy haze and the nearly pitch-black room. He counted seven intruders, including two on him, dressed in dark military clothing. They wore full-face tactical masks. *We've been discovered!*

After much scuffling, grunting, as the hazy air settled, a sinister silence commenced. A muscular man, dressed in a suit, wearing a black cap with the UNO embroidered patch, strutted in through the backdoor holding a fancy wooden cane. He sneered at the restrained company, twisting his curled-up mustache.

Benjamin groaned. *Oh, My Lord, Jesus! It cannot be. It's Abdul Mohammad, the current Prime Minister of UNO, and my former Lieutenant Colonel.*

Abdul poked Morris with his cane. "It is with great pleasure that I get to see you again, my friend. How long has it been, two decades, eh? How's the leg?"

"Get over yourself." Benjamin sucked in his breath, and shot off a thick wad of saliva.

Mohammad wiped the spit from his suit jacket. "I vowed to never stop searching for you after you got away. And here we are. What a beautiful feeling."

Benjamin shuddered at the grim reality. He had successfully eluded Abdul Mohammad for almost twenty years. Abdul was Howard Rohls' replacement. *How could we have been discovered? God, I've been your faithful servant all this time, doing Your will. Please, don't take this away. We're so close. What is going to happen to us? These beautiful Jesus disciples.*

Morris straightened up, "Leave us alone, what crime have we committed?"

"What crime? Let's see what we have here?" Abdul fumbled through Benjamin's briefcase and grabbed a clipboard containing pages of tasks for each of the members, biblical scriptures, and notes on anti-government warfare. The captor tossed the clipboard to the floor, dug further into the bag and yanked out another letter, belting out a menacing laugh.

Glancing over at Benjamin, he said, "This is interesting. Looks like Bible study and a little sharing of your sibling's sob story right before you killed him, Sammy?"

Petra was confused. *Sammy? Who's Sammy?*

"Ahh …," Jacob growled while pinned against the wall. *I knew something was off.*

Mohammad squawked. "Oh, they don't know. What have you *not* shared with these youngsters Sammy Quinn, or should I call you SQ? That's your name after all." He ripped the sheet in half and looked at the bound captives. "You don't know much about this man, do you?"

Morris shifted uneasily in his seat. *Stay calm Sammy. Stay calm. I need to think. I need to think.* "What do you want?"

Abdul ignored the question and searched through the carrycase again. Pulling out a heavy Bible, he pitched it at his former captain's face, the spine hit hard against the end of his nose, "Argh…"

Franklin tried wiggling free from the floor. "Sir, what's going on?"

Mohammad grabbed Benjamin's collar. "Listen you, idiot. You are mine! And so is your entourage."

"What's he talking about?" Caleb blubbered.

Abdul smirked and looked to the others, "By your affiliation with this *traitor*, you will all die at my hand!" He turned back and glared at Benjamin. "Now, I will get my revenge for you defecting from UNO. No one! And I mean, no one *ever* leaves UNO, not ever!"

Jacob squirmed under his assailant. *His voice sounds familiar. Where have I heard that voice?*

Blood dripped from Morris' nose, it trickled over his lips, and he spat, "I'm curious. How did you find us? Though, I'm not impressed by how long it took."

Joshua pushed and pulled at his cords. "You know this person, sir?"

Mohammad sneered and took off his cap. "Ah, he knows me, alright. He reported directly to me. I used to be his Lieutenant Colonel."

It's the Prime Minister. I knew it! Jacob growled.

Abdul directed his attention back to the five, "I have to applaud your 'Captain'. It's taken me a while to locate him. I was patient, though. I've moved up in rank. You know, being the Prime Minister, my government role is as powerful as that of President Philip Borsta II."

"Congratulations, I'd clap for you, but my hands are tied. No matter the title, you'll always be someone else's slave, Abdul," Benjamin replied snidely.

Mohammad grinned. "And you're my dead body. I knew your stupidity would be your downfall. UNO has the best military and the most prestigious savvy hackers. We didn't even know until recently about your other groups. We got your location ping from the message you sent to your campers here."

Morris' fists tightened under his restraints. *Breathe Sammy. Breathe.*

Abdul tapped his cane on the floor. "Oh, I also ran into Brian Kraft about nine months ago, remember him?"

Brian? Oh gosh! The man was weak, always complaining about the assignments. Glad he left on his own.

"He told me about being in your group, your fourth one to be exact. He gave me some great insight too. How many teams have you had since?"

Morris shook his head. *I knew I couldn't trust him.* "… None of your business."

Mohammad poked Benjamin in the stomach, hard. "Well, whatever the case, he's been disposed of."

Benjamin grimaced. He gazed wearily at his young warriors. Petra was bound and gagged, tears streaming down her cheeks. Franklin and Caleb were pinned on the floor. Joshua was triple-bound and constricted; Jacob was flattened against the wall. He had lied to them about who he really was and what he did while in UNO, persecuting and killing Christians, Muslims and Jews. Thousands died at his hands as result of him wanting to save his own life. *I'm sorry, Jesus. I was trying to make it up to you, make everything right again all these years. I was going to tell them who I was and come clean. I really was, Lord.*

He and his crew were going to die at the hands of a very evil UNO government official. If only they could escape somehow and continue their goal of resurrecting the Christian faith in the former United States, otherwise, five innocent lives—five enthusiastic lives would be expunged. They returned his gaze with fear. *I have to say something. Come on Holy Spirit; tell me what I need to say …. All for You.*

A memory breezed into his mind. Morris recalled this group's born-again conversion. Three weeks into their initial meetings, in an abandoned warehouse, he baptized each member in a water-filled horse trough, washing away their sins, their pasts, and directing them to accepting Jesus Christ as their Lord and Savior. It was a glorious emotional affair with a touch of silliness, especially when Joshua burst from the water flexing his bulging muscles. But his most treasured baptism went to Petra. She trembled and sobbed while stepping into the trough, and then she came out praising her Heavenly Father. *Yes, Jesus. Yes, Jesus. That's my confirmation. They will be with You in eternity.*

Benjamin cleared his throat. "Don't be afraid. Our physical flesh will be no more, but for what we have accomplished together thus far, we will be rewarded in eternity with our Lord and Savior, Jesus Christ. Remember, Stephen, the first martyr, the Apostle Paul, and countless other martyrs that have sacrificed for OUR FAITH—"

"Shut up, you moron," Abdul growled and slapped Benjamin, but he shook it off. "—Remember Daniel? This is our Shadrach, Meshach, and Abednego moment, don't—" He was slapped again, stunned to silence.

"Your so-called Jesus operation is over. You will burn in *your* hell." Mohammad directed his assailants to move Caleb, Jacob and Franklin to their chairs and bind them like Petra and Joshua.

Benjamin lowered his head. "Father, take this cup away from us, and do a miracle for us. Make a way!"

"Your God will not save you and your friends because there is no God!"

Franklin looked around, strategizing how he and the others could escape. *There has to be a way out.* Each militant was heavily armed. Abdul called one of the guardsman at the backdoor. "Get the gasoline. This crappy shack and its occupants are going up in flames."

"Yes sir," the guard dutifully replied and ran out the back. Mohammad turned toward another militiaman standing at the window, "You, get the camera. We're going to videotape their flesh burning for all to see and show the public what it means when you go against UNO."

"No—" Petra muffled a scream.

Morris raised his head, "It's all for God's glory. Your faith and your work have not been done in vain! Don't forget—"

Abdul slapped Benjamin another time, backhanded, "… Stupid man." He then licked his lips, eyeing the restrained prisoners. "He suckered you all in, like some missionary quest spreading *your* religion. You know what's going to happen to you instead? You're going to burn and die."

"Don't listen to him. This government is evil!" Morris hollered. "Defying Romans 13 is the right thing to do if it's not biblical. When tyranny becomes lawlessness, rebellion becomes Biblical! God is with you. This is just your flesh. Many will be empowered by your sacrifice."

Mohammad laughed at group. "Ha! You're a bunch of idiots if you believe this."

He directed his attention to one of his guards. "And you … Camera ready?"

"Yes, it's all set up."

"Start recording."

The other guardsman reappeared with two large canisters of gasoline, one in each hand.

"You," he said, "begin pouring the fuel over the floor, walls, and then lastly onto these traitors. KASTAM IS THE ONLY RELIGION. We follow ONLY the Visphonice! I want to light the match and get this show taped for the morning news."

Joshua trembled. Beads of sweat appeared on his forehead. *This can't be happening. It can't be.* He recalled an incident with his father when he was a child. He had fallen on the steps and his leg had gotten bruised. His dad was a big man, not very touchy, very aloof. As he sniffled, holding his right leg, his father stomped up to him as a single tear made its way down his cheek. Trembling under his father's glare, he knew his dad hated seeing him cry. He was about to rub his face when his father reached over with his enormous hand and gently wiped the tear away. His dad said, "It's only a scratch, buddy. Don't cry over the small stuff, instead, wail over the big stuff."

Joshua didn't know why that incident had come to his mind. *What does that mean for us?* Droplets flooded his eyes, blinding him; his fists curled up. *Wail over the big stuff. Yes, yes! This was the big stuff. I'm not dying like this.* He flexed his arms and broke free of the cords, knocking down the two guards next to him and lunging at the next closest guard, Caleb's assailant.

"What in the world," Abdul turned, "kill him."

Caleb followed Joshua's lead, pushing, kicking, and eventually breaking free, attacking his assailant, punching him hard in his neck. *Let's fight!*

Jacob ripped through the ties as well and elbowed his guard in the stomach. *We got this!*

Petra started kicking around in her chair. *I've seen too much in Ukraine to not fight back.*

Franklin freed himself and punched his guardsman in the thigh and then on his masked head. *No one treats my mentor like this. NO ONE.*

More militiamen came through the backdoor. The guard with the gasoline joined the brawl, tossing the empty cans aside. The guard with the video camera followed the action. Mohammad slammed his cane on the floor, "Kill them all!"

Bullets fired in all directions until the growling and grunting stopped, and the thudding sounds of bodies dropping to the floor ceased. Abdul stepped forward, "Good job men, we got them all."

Benjamin sat up in his chair. He was the only one still tied, unable to get loose. Blood seeped through his shirt. He coughed, leaning forward, "Correction, *Mr. Prime Minister*, you missed one."

Caleb stood in the doorway of the smoke-filled room. He lit a match and tossed it, flames burst everywhere. "No! —" Mohammad shouted as the fire roared over the hardwood flooring, burning everyone and everything in its path.

With only a few seconds to spare, Caleb snatched a rifle lying on the floor, he noticed Petra's dead body; several rounds penetrated her neck and face. *Oh, my sister in Christ, I'm so sorry we couldn't protect you.*

Fire raged everywhere. He quickly scanned the room for the others. Jacob had wounds in both hands, *his playing card hands*, and in the spine; Joshua, shot multiple times in the chest, his big muscular chest, and Franklin, one clean bullet to his head, his face glowed, as if grinning.

Caleb's knees buckled, but something jerked him upward, and he staggered out the backdoor and into the deserted road, crying out, "Jesus, Jesus, Jesus."

Chapter 6 – The Arrival

August 2033. Bethel, New York.

A little over a year later, in a field of an old dairy farm in Bethel, New York, Caleb stood on a stage behind a small podium made out of a huge stump from a sycamore tree, a donation given by Dr. Laurence in Wyoming for this grand revival.

It should have been Benjamin Morris standing behind this podium. This was his vision. Maybe this was the way it was supposed to turn out. Only God knows.

The young man ran his fingers over the hand-carved wood, remembering when Benjamin told them the biblical story of Zacchaeus, the tax collector in Jericho, how he climbed up a tree to see Jesus walk by, and how the Lord then invited himself to his home. The sycamore tree Zacchaeus climbed symbolized a regeneration of sorts, strength, and divinity. A solid piece of wood, made strong, used as a stepstool to lift a short man up from his evilness to an encountering with the Holy One.

Caleb marveled at the sight of thousands of people standing in the field, the miraculous wonders of what Jesus had done through himself and others who helped organize this event. It was God's providence to assemble all these hungry folks, considering how UNO and KASTAM destroyed the public's faith in God and replaced it with electronic enlightenment, mind tracking, and Pharmakeia (sorcery), as mentioned in Galatians and Revelations. Eyes were opened, scales removed. They were finally seeing through the blindness and ignorance accumulated over the last two decades.

White, fluffy clouds filled the sky, floating in the warm August temperatures. Holding a microphone, with a large screen situated behind him, Caleb addressed the sea of heads, "My name is Caleb, I'm nineteen-years-old and I'm proud to say I am a Christian, and so are all of you." Clapping and whistling rippled through the swarm of attendees. "It's been a remarkable two days seeing all of you getting saved, baptized, born-again. Two Corinthians 5:17 says, if you are in Christ, you are a new creation. Celebrate that!"

More clapping and cheering followed. "This is the third and the final day for this glorious, God-inspiring gathering. I'm grateful for your willingness to change our world." The crowd exploded and Caleb continued once it quieted down. "We are standing on a historical site, one that you might not be aware of because the history of the USA, as we knew it, was erased. I am holding," he lifted a book in the air, "a book about our history. In August of 1969, sixty-three years ago, in this very field, one of the largest music festivals of our time, *Woodstock*, was held. Over two hundred thousand people attended the three-day event, a festival filled with bands, drugs, and promiscuous sex."

Caleb put the book down and then picked up a Bible, cradling it close to his chest, "Today, we are consecrating this soil, making it holy, pure, and righteous again." More whistles and joyous cries erupted.

"This used to be a 600-acre dairy farm owned by Max Yasgur. During that time, there was a war going on in Vietnam from 1965 to 1973. A lot of American men and women risked their lives for that war; there were a lot of causalities too. For those that came back, they weren't given the respect they deserved. This field was occupied for this short time by many individuals who protested against that war. There was division on both sides, those for and those against the war. It reminds me of what's happened to all of us."

Caleb stopped and surveyed the assembly of new converts, young and old, some former Christians, new Christians, and KASTAM converts who were beaten down by UNO with its tyrannical mandates and rules. All these people yearned for freedom, a restored faith in God, not some ideological spirit and binding set of manipulating regulations on the body, mind, and soul.

"There is no purpose to living except what UNO tells us to do. It is because our faith and worship in Jesus Christ that had been removed altogether. KASTAM is unfulfilling! With you all here," he pointed to the crowd, "this is a grassroots effort, doing what God our Father would have wanted us to do. Go out and minister, witness to non-believers and convert them to Christ-followers."

Caleb waved his Bible in the air, "One Peter 3:15 tells us this … *'But sanctify the Lord God in your hearts, and always be ready to give a defense to everyone who asks you a reason for the hope that is in you with fear and weakness.'*"

He paused and ran his hand along the edges of the podium. "I tell you now, you will be persecuted, maybe verbally, or worse. Jesus said in Matthew 10: 22-24, *'And you will be hated by all for My name's sake. But he who endures to the end will be saved. When they persecute you in this city, flee to another. For assuredly I say to you, you will not have gone through the cities of Israel before the Son of Man comes.'* I promise you this, the rewards of eternal life in Heaven are much greater than you can ever imagine."

Cheers, whistles, and clapping continued. Caleb was overwhelmed with the people's enthusiasm. He steadied himself, holding the podium tightly. Closing his eyes, he could still see the images of his teammates and leader who had been killed on that fateful night, the one night that changed everything for him and the thousands in attendance at this revival.

Chapter 7 – The Handwritten Notes

Gunfire ensued and bodies were pushed and shoved about. Caleb dropped to the floor and crawled toward Morris, seeing Franklin close by. He overheard their conversation …

"—Inside my—case—take the—keys, the Bible—," Morris said, his voice raspy, "sorry—let you down, Franklin."

"—I'm not leaving you, sir," he gibbered, holding back a dam of tears while trying to untie his leader from the chair. *I can't leave you. You've given me new life, an opportunity to return to Jesus. I have to save you.* He recalled what his mentor had told him at the construction site months earlier where they had met, "Man may have forsaken you. Your father may have erred, but God will never leave you. Your knowledge of buildings will be very useful."

Reality jolted Franklin from his thoughts just as Benjamin scolded, "—page 97—Go now—"

Caleb reached them and crouched. "Franklin, let me help you and—"

Franklin turned, "—Get down!"

Caleb shrank to the floor as bullets missed his left shoulder, hitting Morris in the chest. He howled, "No—"

Another gunshot struck Franklin between his eyes, shattering his frames. He fell backwards, the briefcase dropped to the floor with a thud.

Benjamin sputtered, "T-t-take keys—g-g-grab Bi—ble—p-p-page 97—"

Caleb spun around, snatched the carrycase and Bible, slipped down on the floor again, and crawled, gaping at the gruesome sight of his fallen comrades until he got to the doorway. *Oh my God! I can't.* On the verge of vomiting, his legs stood up and robotically dragged him out of the house.

Caleb gripped his leader's bag in his hand and sprinted down the darkened road and into the forest, walking for hours, keeping away from the main roads until daylight. Cold and tired, he saw an abandoned shack and cautiously made his way there, breaking one of the windows and climbing in. A musty smell permeated the air, a few fat rats scurried about. He collapsed on the dirty, linoleum-checkered floor and just bawled. *They're all gone. Gone! How can I be the only one alive and they're all dead?*

Less than a few hours ago he was checking the perimeter with muscle-boy Joshua, trying to protect Petra from the world, making sandwiches with Jacob, receiving encouragement from Franklin on being fearless, and feeling accepted by their beloved teacher for his onslaught of questions. And then, it was over.

A half-hour passed and Caleb wiped his wet face on his shirt. He closed his eyes and took several deep breaths trying to piece together his dire situation.

Jumping to his feet he paced, "What do I do? What do I do? I don't know what to do, God!"

Marching back and forth he accidentally kicked Benjamin's tan briefcase. "Ouch!" *The briefcase! What's in this bag?* Caleb slumped to the floor and looked inside. He pulled a few items out. One of them was a torn yellowed sheet of paper, similar to the old pages Benjamin had been reading to them. *It must be another one of Dennis' letters. The writing looks the same.* He flipped it over and read …

The year is 2012, December twelfth to be exact. It is a Saturday afternoon. I sit in my office in a high rise overlooking what was once Lake Michigan. It is now a dead body of water, like an oil pit. My subordinates call me Major. Major of what?

I have done my duty for the past four years, and been rewarded generously with women and money. But I am soiled with all the evil work I've done.

Today is my birthday. I can't even remember how old I am. My life has been wasted. I did what they wanted. I turned my back on God far too long. I cannot live with myself like this. I'm done. He's coming fo ...

The rest of the page was ripped. *The Prime Minister must have torn the sheet. Where's the rest of this letter?* Caleb shook the contents out of the briefcase to see if there was anything else. "Who's coming for Dennis?"

A Bible lay on the floor. He picked it up and opened it. It was a 2003 New King James edition. On the third page was a handwritten name: Dennis Lee Quinn. *This is Dennis' Bible! Why did Benjamin have Dennis' Bible?* Then, turning to page 97, in the Book of Numbers, he found a white envelope taped to the page. *What is this?* Caleb pulled the envelope off carefully, tore the flap open and removed a few handwritten pages.

My Faithful Jesus Warrior,

My name is Sammy Quinn. I go by SQ. I am the twin brother to Dennis Lee Quinn ...

Caleb slapped his leg, "Are you kidding me? Sammy and Dennis were brothers?" *That's what that evil man had implied to Benjamin at the house regarding the letter.* "Why did he tell us his name was Benjamin Morris? Oh my gosh, this revelation is unbelievable."

I took a gamble. Caleb, whatever the outcome that led you to read this, know it had to be you. Yes, you. That's what the Holy Spirit downloaded into my spirit. Remember the story I told you, two meetings ago, about The Faithful Servant and the Evil Servant in Luke 12:35-48? As followers of Christ, we need to be ready when the Master comes home. His servants were waiting and kept watch. I've been preparing you in these teachings. You are ready. I thank God that he chose you. You will rekindle Christianity.

Caleb stopped and wept, "What? Rekindle?" *Why am I the lone survivor? No, no, no! What am I supposed to do? I'm only eighteen-years-old!* Wiping his eyes, he read some more.

From the moment I recruited you, I knew you were destined for bigger things. Your name is strong. Caleb was a faithful man of God. You can read all about him in Numbers. That's why I taped the envelope to that particular book in the Bible. Nothing is coincidental with the Lord.

God had used Caleb to help Moses after the Israelites were freed from Egypt and wandered in the wilderness for forty years. All the wicked generations had died, only Joshua and Caleb lived on. Through his old age, Caleb persisted and pursued God. Do you know your name comes from the word 'dog'? Caleb never wavered and was as tenacious as a dog can be. You will prosper and do the work set before you.

As for me, I hope you can understand. My heart was hardened way too long. But God kept chipping away at me, took my heart of stone and made it a heart of flesh as it is written in Ezekiel 36:26.

Dennis was a good son, a great husband and father, strong, never wavering in his convictions. James 1:6-8 reminds us to not be double-minded in our convictions, beliefs, and spirit. My brother was all that and more. Me, I vacillated. It's all I had known. And I murdered him in 2012 to gain worldly power. Fortunately, God had other plans for me, and thankfully, like Saul of Tarsus, as described in the Book of Acts, who became the Apostle Paul, I too had a conversion and changed my name from Sammy Quinn to Benjamin Morris.

Caleb stopped again, running a hand down his face. *What is all this? I don't understand how this came to be.* He turned the page.

I've already told you all about me leaving the States to go to Afghanistan in 2008. When I returned, UNO was devouring every city and state like a behemoth. In an instant everything that I had known was gone. I was told to either join UNO and live, or die. I chose the former. To do so, I had to show them I was aligned with the government by capturing or killing any remaining kin.

I went to Chicago to find my wife and daughter, but they'd been captured. Dennis was the only one left. I located him downtown and apprehended him. UNO hoped to convert him from his ridiculous religion, since he was a born-again Christian. Dennis complied, but he was never the same. He became robot-like, dead inside. I, on the other hand, found a new thriving occupation, killing woman, men, children of all religious denominations, especially, Christians.

A bright light crossed Caleb's face; he put his hand out, noticing the sun was rising. He went over and peered out the dusty window. *So, Sammy and Dennis were part of UNO? I looked up to Benjamin. Why did he lie to us? What if UNO finds me?*

He looked around the house. It had already been ransacked of anything worthy, no running water either. He ambled over to what resembled a bathroom and relieved himself. Collecting the pages again, Caleb read.

While I was out in the field on my mass killing spree, Dennis, with his corporate business savvy and keen sense of numbers, got a cushy position working within the government keeping crypto money for bioweapons in balance. UNO kept tabs on him. My brother despised me, he often told me I was living in absolute sin. And soon, he'd escape.

This fueled my anger even more than my desire for power. I wanted approval from my newly appointed Lt. Col., Abdul Mohammad. In my foolishness, I confessed my brother's next steps to him. Abdul saw something in me that my own father never saw in me, desperation, and he took advantage of it. Abdul ordered me to kill Dennis, but not right away. At the moment he was an important asset. I had no choice but to obey.

I regretted this assignment because I was stuck. I hoped Dennis continued to be of value to UNO for a long time, I honestly wasn't ready to kill my kin, no matter how much I hated him.

After four years, my brother made a dire mistake and UNO discovered he was holding men's Bible study. He became a liability. The pressure was on me to do the deed. So, in 2012, I went to Dennis' office while he was working, and I killed him.

Caleb threw the papers on the floor. He couldn't believe their God-fearing leader murdered his own blood. *That's what the sentence in Dennis' letter was referring to; it was Sammy aka Benjamin who was coming for him.* Disappointment and anger welled up in his gut.

"Why did you do that, Sammy? You are a terrible person!" Frustrated, he stood and marched about, almost striking one of the rats in his path. He imagined how that interaction could have gone.

DENNIS FOLDED HIS LAST LETTER. *This should do it. They will know the truth about the seizures that happened in Chicago. Insignificant as I am, they'll also know my story from my other letter. My faith in Jesus is much, much bigger. There's no trading a life in eternity for a life in this world.*

It was Saturday and he was the only one in the office. Lieutenant Colonel Mohammad had wanted him to go over some special financials right away. The military needed additional trucks and equipment. These numbers would be taken to the higher-ups for approval or disapproval.

When he was finished, Dennis arose and looked out of his twentieth-floor window overlooking the streets below. Armies of men were on patrol. Taking a sip of water, he cheered himself in the reflection, "Happy birthday to me."

Turning, he grabbed his camouflaged-covered Bible, getting ready to bury this letter with the others he had hidden a few years back. Someone knocked, Dennis stiffened as he slowly slipped back into his chair. "Come in."

The door slowly opened and Sammy, his twin, strolled in dressed in a military uniform, minus a few less patches and medals than his honored sibling.

"Hi Dennis," he greeted, removing dark-colored sunglasses.

"What brings you here, SQ?"

Sammy closed the door and inched forward, "Business, *unfinished business.*"

Dennis folded his arms and leaned forward. "It's been, what, four years. Guess I've been waiting and preparing for this day, you know? It's our birthday brother, so happy birthday to you."

Sammy took a chair across from him, the two siblings ogled one another. "Yes, it's our birthday alright, happy birthday to you too." He looked around. "You've done great work for UNO, you know, keeping the money in balance. I'm not surprised you've done this well. But, since you made a mistake, Lieutenant Colonel Mohammad is finished with you."

Dennis smirked, "So be it. I did what I was supposed to do. I had no choice, not after you almost choked me out in Grant Park. You could have let me go."

SQ laughed, "Why? It was fun torturing the 'golden son'. And, you've always been respected, no need to work your butt off like me. You've always had it easy. Even Mom and Dad adored you more than me."

Dennis took another sip of water. "I don't understand why you've always been jealous of me. What did I do to you?"

Sammy's smile faded, "You *existed.*"

"You don't have to do this. We could disappear, go off-the-grid. They'll never catch us," Dennis pleaded. "My dear brother, you need Jesus. Please, don't. Together we can help so many people come to Christ."

SQ's face changed to one of anger. He rose from the seat and drew his Colt M1911. "You and your silly Jesus. All of UNO knows about your ridiculous beliefs."

Dennis shook his head, facing his executioner. "I pray you will repent and turn from your wicked ways. Jesus is the only way, Sammy. He loves you. And I love you too."

Sammy flinched, shaking off the comments as if he were swatting flies.

His brother stood up. "I forgive you for what you're about to do."

Pointing the gun toward his twin's head, Sammy fired once. Dennis' body arched back into his chair; calmness blanketed his face as his eyes rolled up in his head. *The job is completed.* SQ gathered his brother's belongings and marched out of the office.

CALEB STOPPED ROAMING AROUND, collected the strewn pages, and organized them again. He squatted to the floor, finding where he'd left off, and continued reading.

I didn't have one ounce of regret. I know it sounds insane, but I was. It makes me think of the story of Cain and Abel in Genesis 4 when Cain confronted his brother, full of jealousy and rage, killing Abel in the field. Why? Because God loved Abel's offering better than Cain. And I killed my only sibling because the 'world' loved Dennis more than me.

Among his things, I found the letter he'd just written before I'd murdered him with revelations to another letter he'd written in 2008 about the UNO takeover in Chicago, and where they were located. Dennis must have known his time was almost up. He must also have known it would be me, he said so himself.

I collected his letter, took his Bible, and went to Grant Park. I found the clearing where Dennis buried his backpack, dug it up, and inserted that page along with the others, burying them again, to forget, and erase his existence forever.

Years went by while I was in hiding. I couldn't shake the thought of those letters, or my brother. I returned to Grant Park, dug up the backpack and kept them all this time. My wife died and my daughter and grandson haven't seen me in over a decade. They don't believe I'm still alive. It's better for them. I'm a sinful wretched man!

I'm a liar for never being honest and truthful with my past. I wanted to confess to you and the others. And I would have because Dennis Lee Quinn was a good man, a true believer! I took those letters as a constant reminder of the sinner I was until ... let me explain further.

A few weeks after Dennis' murder, I was working alone, investigating a storage facility to clear anything, like civilians hiding out from UNO. However, while checking the grounds, I found a child, a boy maybe nine-years-old. It looked like he'd been hiding there a while. He had been eating dead rats.

The first thing I noticed was a rusty chain with a cross dangling from his thin neck. Oh, how my anger resurfaced. Then, a darn Bible lay on the floor. More anger. He pointed a homemade rifle at me. After I coaxed him into believing I'd let him go, I pulled out my gun and fired three times, with no remorse. Afterwards, I checked the rest of the grounds, got into my truck, and drove away. Just another day on the job, killing believers.

While driving, the steering wheel locked, and I lost control of my truck. I hit a large willow tree, a thick branch broke off and crashed on top of the truck, crushing the roof, barely missing my right arm.

I managed to push open the driver's side door and I tumbled out, the seatbelt got hooked on my right ankle and I couldn't shake it free. I smelled gas, so I hurried. A small fire had started on the dashboard. I sensed the vehicle was going to blow up in minutes. Wriggling and struggling to get loose, a flash of light hovered over me and blinded me. I swear I saw that boy standing over me, his brown face was streaked with tears.

Shocked, I froze. My foot had loosened, I pulled away, hobbling and limping just as the truck exploded. I had survived, but something changed in me, and even though it sounds cliché, from that day on, I vowed to give my life to Christ and rouse those who are without faith. I was getting out of UNO.

While at that political rally, I was filled with something so strong that I started protesting against it. They seized me and I was severely beaten, my left leg was injured so badly I could never walk properly again, not to mention the constant pain. Luckily, I escaped. Like Jacob in Genesis, whose hip was broken, I've carried this infirmity, a reminder of what brought me to this new life in Jesus Christ.

Caleb, I'm deeply sorry for all the hurt I've caused. I hope you can forgive me of my transgressions. Please continue with our evangelical purpose, but more importantly, I want you to go bigger in reaching the masses by holding a revival. You're going to do it in New York City. This is what I'd been preparing and prepping this group for. Go to Taos, New Mexico first. I have a cousin there who can equip you with all the details and plans I have documented. Don't delay.

Remember Matthew 13:23, 'But he who received seed on good ground is he who hears the word and understands it, who indeed bears fruit and produces: some a hundredfold, some sixty, some thirty.' You hold the thirty-fold.

Grace be with you,

Benjamin Morris (The Rekindler) 2 Timothy 1:6-14

Chapter 8 – The Prophesy

After Caleb's harrowing exodus from the hands of Abdul Mohammad and his militia, getting to New Mexico was no easy feat. Dying his hair black and growing a stubble of a beard on his young face, he looked a few years older, but he didn't care; he was alive, a fugitive on the run. God's hand was upon him. Stopped for questioning three times, he pretended to hail UNO and recited content from the Visphonice.

After weeks of traveling by auto, railway, and hitchhiking, Caleb eventually made it to Benjamin's cousin's house. A tiny, two-bedroom, one bath ranch with a roof made out of sun-dried clay bricks, situated at the end of a pebbled dead-end street. The closest neighbor was several 'city-blocks' away. The young man introduced himself to Col. Bill Medalion, a former decorated Marine.

Using Morris' keys, Caleb unlocked a rusted silver chest in the attic of the home. Inside, he found several handwritten notebooks, instructions for a revival.

Caleb spent three months pouring over strategies about how to commence this impossible undertaking, transcribing all the notes into a manual, and then assembling a willing crew dedicated to winning souls for Jesus.

During this time, one question nagged him. *Why did Sammy change his name?* One night, he mentioned the issue to the Colonel.

Medalion was in the kitchen making coffee. He lived alone. He was a tall, balding man, and still very muscular at almost seventy. Bill's mother and Dennis and Sammy's mom were sisters, hence the cousin connection.

Bill had effectively avoided capture by UNO all these years. Caleb wanted to ask him how he had done that and why he lived by himself, but he thought better of it. The man, over six and a half feet tall, had a frightening demeanor about him.

Caleb, however, needed to learn the significance of Benjamin's name. A discussion ensued. It was after nine, and he decided to take a break after spending an hour writing notes. The aroma of coffee led him to the kitchen. "Smells good," Caleb remarked, sitting down at the table for two.

Bill gazed out of the window over the sink. Without turning he said, "Yes, it does. Figured you could use something to keep your mind sharp."

Caleb smiled, "I appreciate it, sir. I also appreciate you allowing me to stay here and go over all the documents Benjamin, I mean Sammy, had put together."

Medalion faced him, "It's alright, son. His name is Benjamin. Good and bad, he earned it, his new namesake."

The young man leaned over the table. "I've been meaning to … that is, I'm curious about Sammy's name change to Benjamin Morris. Can you enlighten me?"

Bill filled two cups and joined him. "Sure, I wondered when you'd ask. I'll take it you can guess there was some animosity between the brothers by now?"

Caleb took a couple of sips. "Yes, I've gleaned that from Benjamin's letter."

Medalion tapped at his mug. "It was some time after Dennis passed that Benjamin, formerly Sammy made his way down here." The man exhaled, "Benjamin was a mess, physically and spiritually."

Caleb cupped his hands around his mug, "How long did he stay with you?"

The Colonel sipped. "… About a year. He wanted to change. Killing that little boy and dodging death from the truck, had really screwed up his psyche. He needed time to heal from the beatings too. Benjamin confessed saying, of all the thousands he'd murdered, men, women, and children, that child's murder was the one that broke his back like the proverbial straw. God was right in doing so."

Medalion paused for a moment. "I'm a believer in Christ and I read the Bible every single day. Sammy had Dennis' Bible, and with my encouragement, together, we started reading it nightly to destroy the demons consuming him. The man needed repentance to change his life and get right with God because He was going to use Sammy for His glory."

Caleb got up from the table. "I have Dennis' Bible with me, I'll get it." Grabbing it from the bedroom, he brought it to the table.

Bill picked it up in admiration. "Yep, this is the one. Anyhow, we started reading the story of Jacob and Rachel in the Book of Genesis. Jacob had twelve sons, the twelve tribes of Israel. Jacob had two sons born by his wife, Rachel. One was Joseph, whom he loved so much, and his brothers betrayed him. The other was a baby boy, Benjamin. Rachel died in childbirth and before she passed, she named him Ben-oi, which means 'son of my pain or son of my sorrow'. Jacob later changed his son's name to Benjamin which means 'son of my right hand'. Sammy felt he represented the son of sorrow and Dennis, his twin brother, the son of the right hand, even though Benjamin, son of Jacob, was the same person embodied as was told in the Bible. And so, he made the decision to change his name as an atonement of his sins, killing all other denominations, especially Christians because in Genesis 49:27, when Jacob is blessing all his sons, he says this about Benjamin … *'Benjamin is a ravenous wolf; in the morning he devours his prey, and at night he divides his spoil.'* How about that?" the Colonel concluded, sitting back.

Caleb drained his coffee. "What a prophecy. That's exactly what Sammy did prior to his conversion; he killed citizens of all faiths, especially Christians in the name of KASTAM."

Bill nodded. "Little did SQ know that by doing that, he changed the fate of his own future with his name."

"There's more?"

"Yes, we read about Benjamin and the Tribe of Benjamin, the Benjamites, which ensued his prophesy, there are many interesting characters that hail from this tribe in scripture. They were a mighty military, you have Saul, the first King of Israel, and Queen Esther from Persia. But the most notable of *this* Tribe of Benjamin was, Saul of Tarsus the converted apostle, Paul."

The younger man's mouth dropped, "Wow!"

Bill laughed, "Wow, huh? One of the things Sammy learned about himself was to repent of all the sins he committed. You see, he devoured and killed hundreds of people of faith every day, like Saul. When Saul became Paul, he was redeemed of his sins, and ended up writing fourteen books of the Bible. These groups Benjamin had started were his redemption."

Caleb, overcome with emotion, put his head on the table and bawled. *I can't imagine all the pain Benjamin Morris carried. How am I going to carry my mentor's legacy? How am I alone going to resurrect the Christian faith and convert the masses to Jesus?*

Medalion handed him a few tissues, "Here you go."

Caleb blew his nose, "I'm sorry."

"That's what they all say."

Caleb laughed and together they sat in silence for a bit. "Where does 'Morris' come from?"

Bill shrugged, "I don't know. Maybe it sounded good to go along with his first name."

Both men chuckled. Caleb opened the Bible to 2 Timothy 1:6-14 and started reading. Stopping, he remembered Benjamin had signed the letter to him with the phrase, 'The Rekindler'. He raised his head. "What's a 'Rekindler'?"

Medalion rubbed his hands together. "That's who Sammy was, someone who stirs something up again, something that's been dead. Like the story of Lazarus in John 11 when Jesus brought him back to life. Sammy or Benjamin, desired to bring back this spiritual stirring of a renewed and restored faith in Christ Jesus for all of us."

Caleb shifted in his chair. "… Seems very fitting with the name Benjamin. I like the Lazarus story analogy too. Hmm, he always stressed his desire to grow organically. I know now he had plenty of failed teams. I don't want to fail him, either."

Bill tapped his fingers on the table. "You won't."

Caleb was pensive for a moment. The images of his colleagues came into his mind. "He … he really sparked a fire in all of … of us."

Medalion reached across the table and fist-bumped him, "It's fine. I feel your loss."

The young man pointed to the words on the page, and exhaled loudly. "I really like these verses in 2 Timothy. It talks about stirring up the gifts that God has given us. Benjamin had a gift. He wanted to tell the whole world about Jesus without any fear."

"Yep he did. Those are some powerful verses. But you also have a gift. Look what you've done with Benjamin's instructions by organizing his notes and instructions, and rewriting them."

Caleb shrugged. "I guess it did need some reworking. I want to do right. I appreciate that these verses also talk about not being ashamed, and giving testimony to the Lord. I survived an almost horrific capture, it had to be divine intervention."

The Colonel smiled. "That's definitely your testimony and story to tell others. You were brought on board to complete a heavenly mission. Don't discount that."

"Thanks for that," Caleb commented. "The last line of this entire verse is something to ponder on. Allowing the Holy Spirit to dwell in us. How do I know I even have the Holy Spirit in me?"

Medalion clasped his hands. "That's for you to discover. For now, you have a better understanding of who Sammy identified with, where his name came from, his goals, and his fondness for the Apostle Paul through the lineage of the Benjamites."

Caleb stood up, put his coffee cup in the sink, and turned around. "You're right about that. If only this wasn't such a big undertaking."

Bill faced the younger man. "I know it's big. I trust God with all my heart. I think Benjamin knew you could do it too. You have been chosen, son. He bequeathed you a flame. Steward it well. Now go and rekindle the lost, fire 'em up'!"

A few weeks later, Caleb left Col. Bill Medalion's home to connect with a few of Morris' well-known contacts, including Dr. Lawrence and his team, a dozen of Jacob's poker friends from Canada, and few of Joshua's associates in the media. Together, they began planning for the event. Caleb journeyed all over the US, spending many weeks spreading the Good News, talking about the big gathering taking place in Bethel.

It was during this missionary crusade that Caleb realized his mentor's vision. His understanding had come full circle. Benjamin Morris was preparing them for a Book of Acts revival just like the disciples and many converts had done reaching the lost with the Gospel.

Could this next operation steer the people away from KASTAM, and set ablaze a desire to learn the life and truth of Jesus Christ. He had to try.

Chapter 9 – The Great Plan

Caleb pressed a button on a remote control, the big screen flashed photos of his former teammates: Petra, Joshua, Franklin, Jacob, and Benjamin Morris. He pointed to them, "Those were my friends. Each one of them was a representative of you and me. Their desire and sacrifice for living out their faith is a testament to why we need to share the living words of God to the world. This rally is in remembrance of them, but also in honor of our Lord and Savior, Jesus Christ. Are you with me?"

The crowd went ballistic. Caleb put his hand to his ear. "I can't hear you!" The multitude screamed again. "Good. I have a few gentlemen standing behind me. Each of them is going to divide you up into several groups and help you select a leader. That chosen leader will be responsible for disseminating materials and information to the individuals in your assigned group." Impatience rippled through the masses out in the field.

Caleb raised his hand, "Hold up, everyone. Don't worry. My men have a checklist for the leaders to follow. It's okay. Once we are organized, I will share our goals and what you need to do when you go out and evangelize. In Acts 2, when all the people assembled after Pentecost, everyone was in one accord and filled with the Holy Spirit. We need to invite the Holy Spirit to dwell in each one of us for our next steps. Are you still with me?"

"Yes, yes, yes," the masses chanted.

He directed his attention to the men behind him. "You ready?"

"Yes!" they answered in unison. Caleb pumped his fist. "Alright guys, let's get organized."

The men made their way through the crowd and started dividing the participants in groups of fifty. Caleb grinned, watching the many people gathered, starving for the Word of God. That horrific fateful night when he almost lost his life would never be far from his mind. The burden and responsibility sometimes felt like a thick chain around his neck. *I want to fulfill Benjamin Morris' calling. Making sure it continues.*

When all the groupings had been assembled, Caleb took the microphone again. "—I want to share something important. There was once a man named Jonathan Edwards, a preacher and revivalist in his time, who lived from 1703 to 1758. Yes, that's a long time ago, I know. A revivalist is someone who promotes and restarts a spiritual awakening of sorts, similar to what we are doing here."

Caleb continued, "Anyhow, Johnathan Edwards preached about repentance of sin and returning to God. He wrote a sermon entitled: *'Sinners in the Hands of an Angry God'* published in 1741. It was an essay rebuking the people of his time, using a Biblical story about the Israelites and their falling away from God as an example, written in Deuteronomy 32:35, which says: *'Their foot shall slip in due time.'*"

The crowd gasped, Caleb retorted, "That's harsh, I know. Mr. Edwards preached about God's wrath on a wicked and evil people. UNO and KASTAM are both pure evil! Make no mistake, *'Their foot shall slip in due time.'* We need to go out and help our fellow neighbors and citizens turn from their wicked ways, to repent, and come to Jesus. This is our race now. As the Apostle Paul said in 2 Timothy 4:7, *'I have fought the good fight. I have finished the race. I have kept the faith.'* It's our turn to do our duty. So, let us finish this race set before us."

The crowd cheered him on. Caleb realized it could take years for such a monumental transformation, but he also knew it had taken years for Jesus' disciples, equipped with the Holy Spirit, to travel and preach the Good News. This was the same thing.

Caleb signaled to the men. "Hand out the materials to their selected leaders."

As the helpers got to work, Caleb recognized a tall, older man pull away from one of the groups and approach the stage with a teenage boy. A big smile spread across his face as he trotted to the end of the stage and climbed down the stairs. He hugged the man. "Colonel Medalion! What are you doing here?"

Benjamin's cousin returned the embrace and shook the younger man's hand. "I wouldn't miss this for the world. You did it! You really did it! Look at all these Christ followers. It's amazing."

Caleb sighed and gazed at the sea of heads feeling a flutter of joy in his stomach. "It wasn't easy but I'm grateful, very grateful. It wasn't all me. I had a lot of help."

Bill lightly punched him in the arm. "… *'All things work together for good to those who love God.'* That's Romans 8:28. When you have Jesus at the center of your life, He always makes a way."

Caleb radiated, "It means a lot. Thank you."

Medalion turned to the teenager next to him. "Caleb, I'd like you to meet someone."

The boy was almost as tall as Bill. He had a dark brown crew cut, piercing green eyes, and an acne filled chin. He extended his hand. "I'm Frederick, Sammy Quinn's grandson, nice to meet you."

Both shook hands and Caleb stepped back, "Wait, you're the four-year-old grandson? Sorry."

Medalion snickered.

Frederick shrugged, "Yeah, that was me. I'm almost fifteen now."

Caleb touched the teen's arm. "Your grandfather was an impressive man, a great mentor and friend."

Frederick beamed while nudging Bill, "So I've heard."

Caleb fidgeted. "So, how did you hear about this? How did this come about? Where have you been? I want to know."

Bill gestured with his hands, "Slow down, son. You have a lot of people counting on you for direction, this young man included; whom by the grace of God is joining this revival with you."

Frederick grinned.

Caleb choked up, words felt jumbled and thick, like wet cement, "I … I don't know what to say. Thank … Thank you."

Medalion grabbed his shoulder, "I feel you. Now shoo. You got work to do. We will catch up later."

Caleb saluted the Colonel, and shook Frederick's hand again. *Wow, I can't believe I've just met Benjamin's grandson. God, I don't know what to say except You are amazing!*

The wind stirred again, ruffling Caleb's black-colored hair still hanging over his ears. Suddenly, he heard a whisper … "Good and faithful son, I'm so proud of you. Be a Rekindler."

Feeling a glowing presence of the Lord inside him, and warm embrace from his friends wrapping him like a blanket, Caleb smiled, knowing angels would be beside him every step of the way. *Yes, I am a Rekindler. My friends were Rekindlers. My mentor was a Rekindler. These folks standing on this consecrated ground are Rekindlers.*

To be continued …

Truth may have a price, but a Truth that's kindled righteously sets a blaze.

Discussion Questions

- What is the main theme of the story? Is there one underlying theme or are there more?

- How would you describe Benjamin Morris?

- What are Benjamin Morris' strengths? Weaknesses?

- How would you describe each of the characters in Benjamin's new squad? Petra, Franklin, Joshua, Jacob, and Caleb?

- What makes each of these characters unique? What grounds them? What makes them similar? Or different?

- Religion is always a touchy topic for discussion. Explain your reaction to the story?

- In what Christian genre would you place this tale? Inspirational, Warfare, Evangelical, Revival, Dystopian, etc. Explain why?

- What do you make of Dennis' letter?

- What are your thoughts on the reasoning behind why Benjamin shared Dennis' story?

- What is Benjamin's goal for his group?

- There are scenes in the tale that could be considered "Divine Intervention" (a suspension of disbelief). Can you identify those scenes? What are your thoughts on them?

- Describe Benjamin's conversion. What is your takeaway from that?

- Caleb has been given a huge task. What are your thoughts on how you would manage this undertaking if it were you?

- Define, in your own words, what is a Rekindler?

- What can you do to stir up change within your life, family, community, your job?

- The story doesn't end with "The End". Rather, it ends with "To be continued …" What does that mean to you?

Afterthought

The Ephesians were the first people and church that the Apostle Paul had preached to after his conversion while on the road to Damascus. The Ephesians were such faithful stewards in the Body of Christ.

One of my favorite verses in the Book of Ephesians is **Ephesians 1:18.** Paul is lovingly describing these believers … *"The eyes of your understanding being enlightened; that you may know what is the hope of His calling, what are the riches of the glory of His inheritance in the saints …"*

May your eyes be opened with wisdom, revelation, and knowledge of Him. May your calling be aligned with Jesus' calling because we have an inheritance from our Lord Jesus. Let's not forget that, for the Bible tells us:

- Turn away from our sins and seek the Lord. **2 Chronicles 7:14**
- Have a vocal holiness about you; your speech should be graciously and righteously kindling. **James 3:5**
- Use the gifts that the Lord has bestowed upon you, do not fear, and share your testimony of faith because He dwells in you. **2 Timothy 1:6-14**
- Fulfill the Great Commission. Go out into the world, and tell everyone about Jesus. **Mathew 28:16-20, Mark 16:14-20**

"… Do not be afraid; only believe." ~Jesus *(Mark 5:36)*

Inspiration for Writing this Tale

Inspiration for writing **The Rekindler** has been strongly gleaned from the Bible: The *Book of Acts*, the life of the Apostle Paul and the beginning part of the *Book of Revelation*. Other books have inspired me: *The Left Behind Series* by Tim LaHaye and Jerry B. Jenkins; *Brave New World* by Aldous Huxley; *The New World Order* by A. Ralph Epperson; *1984* by George Orwell; *Jesus Revolution* by Greg Laurie; *The Pursuit of God* by A. W. Tozer.

I wrote the first draft of **The Rekindler** in 2009. The tale takes place in 2032, many years from the original conception. This story is about one man's vision for a revival, a return to God in the backdrop of a one-world government and one-world religion. A story of one man's desire to get it right, do right, and be redeemed by the Lord to do His Will.

It's about the persecution of believers in this day and age, colliding with nations wanting to have worldly power, a one-world religion, controlled by an elite few. It's a book on revival, evangelism, and the power of the Holy Spirit that lives within those who believe.

It's also a tribute to all the past revivalists who have come before us to WAKE US UP and get right with God. There is freedom in the name of Jesus.

I'm often influenced by music when I write a book, short story, or a poem. I'm thankful to God for that inspiration, nudging, prompting to action. Three songs have encouraged me during the writing of this tale: "Only Jesus" and "Desert Road" by Casting Crowns; and "Hosea 10:12" by Corey Russell.

Stay true to your convictions, callings, and always be rooted in your faith.

Acknowledgments

I'm thankful to Jesus Christ, my Lord and Savior, for giving me the wisdom and discipline to write at all and to be His voice and spread His message to the world. This was an ambitious undertaking for me as I've never written this kind of story.

I'm grateful to my husband, Joe, who has always believed in me and my desire to write stories about human complexities. To my growing teenage daughters, Ava and Stella. May you both be rekindled and exhorted to do greater things in life.

I couldn't have enhanced this tale from 2009 after initially resurrecting it in 2022 and then in 2023 without the assistance of my beta-readers: Alison Migala, Ava Talluto (my daughter), Patricia Allvin, Sarah Mae W (Fiverr). I'm so grateful for their honesty and feedback.

To my wonderful editor and friend, Dennis De Rose from Moneysaver Editing, we go back many years. I can always count on his editing expertise. He has helped me make my stories shine each and every time. Last but not least, a big shout-out to Michelle Rene Goodhew from Mundus Media Ink for capturing my vision in this book's cover.

About the Author

"I'm not a bestselling author; I'm just a 'nobody' who uses stories as my communication tool to encourage others to find their purpose."

Chicago-born, a full-time mother and author, Chiara Talluto, is known as the Master Storyteller in her household. She writes Inspirational/Christian drama empowering women to discover their faith, use perseverance to overcome adversity, and become heroes of their own destinies. Chiara has also dabbled in writing middle-grade fantasy-fairy tales to encourage girls in developing strong morals and values, and to always stand up for what is right.

Currently, Chiara is hard at work penning other stories. Her motto is live, laugh and cry. To learn more about Chiara, visit www.chiaratalluto.com.

Check out her other novels:

She Made It Matter: An Inspirational fiction about one woman's fight to regain sobriety, find salvation, and earn forgiveness after years of guilt from being abandoned by her mother and then losing her brother to cancer, a struggle to vanquish the demons of her past and make her life right again.

Love's Perfect Surrender: A Christian romance about a troubled married couple who lose the "us" part of their relationship after a failed miscarriage and stillbirth, until, the miraculous birth of their daughter, born with a congenital limb deficiency, who graces their lives, shaking their core beliefs in hopes of making peace and letting love in.

Petrella, the Gillian Princess is a Middle-Grade fairy tale that interweaves themes similar to The Little Mermaid, Cinderella, Tangled, Sleeping Beauty and Noah's Ark. It's about a courageous young princess who defies rank and authority to follow her heart. It's a story of hope, bravery and triumph. It is meant to be enjoyed by all readers young at heart, but especially aimed at those children who read middle grade fiction: ages 8 –13.

A Tribute to Tulipia is a feel-good story for all ages about a tulip and her family who live in an oasis of tangled vines, brush and shrubs. Bullied and picked on, the reader journeys with the alienated family who never backed down in their fight to unify a changing forest. It is a great lesson and reminder about what it takes to be a true friend, what sacrifice means, to lay down one's life in order to save another, and to always, always *do the right thing* no matter what.